"So what do you think?" Chance asked.

He'd hung several strands of Christmas lights, and Lynn's old house was looking great. He was standing close to her and she could feel the warmth from his body through the down vest he wore. She'd helped him for the past hour and he'd been wonderful with her boys. And okay, the man smelled wonderful.

"Momma, don't ya got yor ears on? What do you think?" Jack asked, tugging on her arm. It was what she always asked him and Gavin when they weren't listening to her.

Boy, where had she been? "Ear one and ear two are both on and ready to do their jobs," she said lightly.

She hoped Chance hadn't noticed her embarrassing lapse. She stole a glance at him. He caught her looking and the wink he gave her said he'd noticed plenty.

Books by Debra Clopton

Love Inspired

*The Trouble with
  Lacy Brown
*And Baby Makes Five
*No Place Like Home
*Dream a Little Dream
*Meeting Her Match
*Operation:
  Married by Christmas
*Next Door Daddy
*Her Baby Dreams
*The Cowboy Takes a Bride

*Texas Ranger Dad
*Small-Town Brides
  "A Mule Hollow Match"
*Lone Star Cinderella
*His Cowgirl Bride
**Her Forever Cowboy
**Cowboy for Keeps
Yukon Cowboy
**Yuletide Cowboy

*Mule Hollow
**Men of Mule Hollow

DEBRA CLOPTON

was a 2004 Golden Heart finalist in the inspirational category, a 2006 Inspirational Readers' Choice Award winner, a 2007 Golden Quill award winner and a finalist for the 2007 American Christian Fiction Writers Book of the Year Award. She praises the Lord each time someone votes for one of her books, and takes it as an affirmation that she is exactly where God wants her to be.

Debra is a hopeless romantic and loves to create stories with lively heroines and the strong heroes who fall in love with them. But most important, she loves showing her characters living their faith, seeking God's will in their lives one day at a time. Her goal is to give her readers an entertaining story that will make them smile, hopefully laugh and always feel God's goodness as they read her books. She has found the perfect home for her stories, writing for the Love Inspired line, and still has to pinch herself just to see if she really is awake and living her dream.

When she isn't writing, she enjoys taking road trips, reading and spending time with her two sons, Chase and Kris. She loves hearing from readers and can be reached through her website, www.debraclopton.com, or by mail at P.O. Box 1125, Madisonville, Texas 77864.

Yuletide Cowboy
Debra Clopton

Steeple
Hill®

Published by Steeple Hill Books™

STEEPLE HILL BOOKS

Steeple
Hill®

Recycling programs
for this product may
not exist in your area.

ISBN-13: 978-0-373-87640-2

YULETIDE COWBOY

Copyright © 2010 by Debra Clopton

www.SteepleHill.com

Printed in U.S.A.

When I am afraid, I will trust in you. In God, whose word I praise, in God I trust; I will not be afraid. What can mortal man do to me?

—*Psalms* 56: 3, 4

This book is dedicated to my home church: Cowboy Church of Leon County. Thank you all so much for your huge hearts! You are changing lives...mine included!

A special thank-you and dedication to our pastor, Tuffy Lofton—you are a cowboy preacher with a true heart for God.

Chapter One

Chance Turner stepped from his truck as country singer Craig Morgan crooned "Small Town USA" on the radio. He was home in Mule Hollow, Texas, which definitely fit the song's positive image of small-town life in the USA. A smile tugging at his lips, he reached into the truck bed for the large box his sister-in-law had instructed him to deliver to the church.

Colorful strings of Christmas lights overflowed from the box. Melody was late for work, she'd said, and didn't have time to deliver the lights to the church secretary. That had been her pretense anyway, but Chance had no illusions about why she'd asked him to run the errand for her. It was the church.

She wanted him to be as near the church as possible. She had hopes that being here would fix "his problem"... if only it were that easy. He could have told her that seeing the church, being on the premises, wouldn't help him. Instead he'd done as Melody asked—it was easier that way. The last thing he wanted to do was talk about his problem.

And he didn't want to think about it either.

Pushing the dark thoughts aside he focused on delivering the lights. He'd get this done, then he'd head back to the ranch, back to the solitude he'd come home to find. Just him and his horse, and the land that had been in his family for six generations. He wasn't the first Turner to contemplate the state of his life riding in the sanctuary of the vast Turner family ranch. Sanctuary—not exactly something he deserved. Not when he couldn't see past the guilt eating at him.

Still, right now he needed what the solitude of the ranch offered him.

He wanted to ride across the pasture, just him and his horse…but, before he could saddle up, he had lights to deliver.

Hefting the box into his arms he strode toward the quaint white church he'd attended off and on for the better part of his youth. His boots crunched on the white rock and his spurs jangled as he headed down the sidewalk toward the office. The squeals of kids' laughter, shrill with excitement, rode the chilly November wind. Chance had just reached the door when, like bulls out of the chute, two small boys pounded around the edge of the building. Trailing behind them was a monster of a dog.

He tried to sidestep the first kid but he was already on a collision course, and the rest was a blur. One-two-three he was hit by the first kid, fighting for balance as the second kid tangled up with them, and the horse of a dog launched himself at the box of lights in Chance's arms. That was the kicker.

Boots up, head back, Chance sailed straight to the ground, landing like a hundred-and-eighty-pound sack of bad luck!

"Oh, my goodness," Lynn Perry gasped when she opened the door of the church office to find her twins and a long-legged cowboy sprawled on the grass. Rushing forward she grabbed Gavin by his belt and hauled him off Chance, setting him to the side where he stood giggling as she reached for Jack. The poor cowboy was on his own with Tiny, though. The big dog was all over him like butter on toast.

"Tiny, get off of him." Lynn grabbed the dog by his collar and tugged. Nothing happened. "Move, Tiny, you big bag of rocks. Come...*on*." The beautiful, slate-gray Catahoula had a pale buff face outlined in rich chestnut. The giant blinked his silver-blue eyes at her, clueless as to what he was doing wrong. After all, he was simply having a great time sitting on top of the new cowboy play-toy.

Looking less than pleased, Chance scowled as he pushed the dog off him.

"Are you all right?" Lynn asked, holding Tiny back when he flopped his tongue out and made a last-ditch effort to swipe the cowboy's face. "I'm so sorry," she said. The last thing she'd expected to find when she'd heard her kids squealing was Chance Turner, rodeo preacher, beneath the pileup of her twin boys and their dog. Poor man was covered in Christmas lights, too.

In the two years that she'd lived in Mule Hollow the handsome preacher had come home only recently to perform his cousin's wedding. But here he sat sprawled on the sidewalk, his serious green eyes looking through the curtain of Christmas lights hanging from his cowboy hat. Thankfully, those gorgeous eyes were crinkling around the edges as his lips turned up in a smile.

"We had a bit of a wreck," he drawled, instantly sending butterflies into flight in her chest.

Startled, she ignored the response. "A wreck?"

"Yeah, Momma," Gavin offered, grinning like an opossum. "We done run him down. Tiny didn't mean to do it."

Jack looked intently up at her. "It was an accident."

She had to smile and Chance did, too. His lips hitched to one side in that signature Turner grin he shared with his three cousins, a bit crooked with a hint of mischief. Her pulse skittered crazily when his eyes met hers in shared humor.

"Well." She swallowed hard, pushing Tiny out of the way and the frog in her throat, too. "I'm certainly glad it was intentional."

He wore a tan insulated jacket, cowboy-cut at the hips. Tall and lean with dark good looks and a strong jawline, he looked especially cute as he tugged the lights off him. At her words he cocked a dark brow.

"I mean, it *wasn't* intentional," she protested.

He chuckled as he rose to his feet in a smooth motion. "I know. I just got in their way when they came around the corner." He shook his head and lights slid to his shoulders—the boys giggled.

Mortified, she went into action and reached for the lights. "Here, let me help." She began untangling the strings of lights, without much success. "I still don't understand. How a big man like you ended up on the ground? I mean, they're little—" Her mouth was saying things her brain was trying to stop.

"Yup, I do tend to be clumsy. My momma used to say the Lord gave me two left feet when He passed them out."

"Oh, dear, I didn't mean to say that." If the man had a clumsy bone in his body her name was Reba McEntire!

He chuckled and the sound made her feel all warm and happy, like drinking hot cocoa—where in the world had her brain gone?

Gavin stepped up. "We just come around the corner, Momma, and *boom,* there he was." He used exuberant hand gestures to help explain the situation.

"We didn't mean to knock him down." Jack shook his dark head, his big blue eyes looking suddenly worried. "You all right, mister? Tiny's sorry."

Tiny was waltzing about them happily.

"I'm fine. But you two sure pack a punch. Are y'all football players? Or maybe your dog is." That won him a round of giggles.

A crimson tide of humiliation crept warmly up her cheeks when Chance's gaze locked with hers.

"I'm so sorry. I can't believe they knocked you off your feet. As big as you are—I mean. Well, you are a man." Most definitely a man, no doubt about that.

His eyes crimped around the edges and it seemed almost as though he could read her thoughts. Her crazy-unable-to-understand-them-herself thoughts! No mistake about it, despite not wanting to be, she was attracted to Chance Turner. Heart-thumpingly, breathlessly attracted. Okay, so she wasn't dead.

"Last time I looked in the mirror I was a man. But you've got two dynamos here. They took me out like pros with the help of their linebacker there."

Tiny sat on his haunches and cocked his big head as if he knew they were speaking about him.

She scanned the cowboy for damage. Though he was a bit rumpled there were no tears in his long-sleeved shirt, no rips in his jeans. "Are you hurt?" she asked anyway.

"My pride is stomped on, but I don't have any broken bones."

Lynn laughed with a mixture of relief and nervousness. "I guess for a former bull rider like you that is a little hard to swallow."

"You're a *bull rider?*" both boys gushed in unison. They loved bull riders. Something she wasn't thrilled about in the least. To Lynn, riding a bull was right up there with swimming in a shark tank.

"I was a bull rider," he said to the boys, then cocked his head slightly toward her. "Have we met?"

Lynn realized her mistake. "No, not exactly. I'm Lynn Perry. I saw you at Wyatt and Amanda's wedding but we weren't introduced. I heard though that you used to be a bull rider before you became a preacher. They need all the prayers they can get," she added, and realized she'd probably stepped on his toes a bit as he stiffened before taking the hand she held out to him.

She was instantly hit by the strength in his large hand as he wrapped it around hers. Warm pinpoints of awareness prickled across her skin at the touch of his calloused palm. In his eyes she saw a spark of recognition—as if he felt the same sensation—she pulled her hand from his as her pulse kicked up a notch.

"It's nice to meet you, Lynn. I'm Chance, but you already know that." If he was startled by her reaction, he hid it well, tugging a strand of lights from his shoulder as if he didn't notice anything out of the ordinary. "I guess these lights are for the church? Melody, my sister-in-law, said I was to bring them here and give them to the secretary. Is that you?"

"That's me." Had Melody meant them for her? They hadn't discussed lights. "I didn't know we were expecting them though."

"Are they *ours?*" Gavin's eyes widened as he looked up at Chance in awe.

"We need some lights, for our house," Jack piped up, beaming at the assortment. "We don't got none do we, Momma?"

Any other time she would have corrected his English but not now. It had been a hard month getting moved from the shelter to the house she was renting. Settling in and making it a home had cost more than she'd planned, and with Christmas right around the corner money was tighter than ever. She'd been saving every penny she could over the last two years while they lived at No Place Like Home, the women's shelter from abuse. Most of her savings had gone toward rent, deposit and getting all the utilities turned on. Christmas lights hadn't been in the budget and yet the boys talked about them all the time. Trying not to dwell on what she couldn't give the boys, she focused on what she had accomplished and quickly moved past the tug of feeling sorry for herself.

She refused to give in to those types of feelings when they snuck up on her. Instead she smiled at the boys.

"Let's pick them up. We'll put them inside the office until I talk to Melody and find out what they're for."

Gavin and Jack whispered to each other, then stared up at Chance.

"You're a preacher?" Jack asked.

Chance hesitated before answering, which seemed odd to Lynn.

"I'm taking a break, but yes, I'm a rodeo preacher." Chance knelt and began rolling up one of the strands of lights into a ball.

Lynn did the same and each boy grabbed a strand of his own, imitating exactly the way Chance was coiling his.

"You boys are doing a great job." Chance flipped the overturned box upright and laid his coiled lights inside. The boys followed suit. They were all grins and eyes full of awe…she understood it. Despite her misgivings, she was attracted to this handsome cowboy. She dropped her lights into the box and gave herself a talking-to— she had no interest in men. Not yet. She'd come a long way since she'd escaped with her sons to the shelter over two years ago, but she hadn't come far enough along to think about bringing a man into the mix. She was building a life with her boys and that was all she cared about doing.

That was what she needed.

Gavin dropped another messy coil into the box, then put his hands on his hips and looked Chance straight in the eyes. "If you're a preacher we need one."

Jack nodded. "In the worstest of ways."

Lynn smiled at his word choice. Jack had heard Applegate Thornton, one of the more colorful older men, saying that at church on Sunday.

"Yeah, the worst," Gavin repeated. "Are you going to fill the puppet?"

Chance laughed in a rich baritone. "No, I'm not preaching right now. I'm taking some time off." The box was full and he picked it up. "Where would you like me to put this?"

She was startled by his answer. "In here." She led the way into the office and he followed her inside as the boys trailed in behind him. She couldn't remember them being so taken by a man before.

He set the box on the table and looked around the office. It was a cozy room with a dark oak desk that gleamed from the polish she applied to it every week. The double bookshelves were full of reference books for a new pastor, who would call this his office when he showed up.

She wondered what Chance thought about the room. He didn't quite fit here. He was too rugged, too masculine—not that a pastor couldn't be both those things. It was simply that *rodeo pastor* fit Chance Turner. "Thank you for bringing the Christmas lights to town," she said, not sure what else to say.

He swept his hat from his head, revealing jet-black hair with a hint of wave. "You're welcome." His gaze was strong and steady as it took her in, causing her pulse to drum faster—despite her will. There was a charge in the room between them that left her breathless. He broke the moment by letting his gaze drift about the office again.

Gathering her wits she took a deep, shaky breath. "It's a bit sad to me." She felt disconcerted by him but tried to seem unaffected. "It just seems wrong for this office not to belong to someone. Ever since Pastor Allen retired we've had a problem finding a pastor who feels called to fill our pulpit."

"That's what I've heard. The right man will come, though," he said, then added, "in God's time."

"Why cain't a rodeo preacher preach here?" Gavin asked, moving to stand right beside Chance so he could look straight up at him.

"They can if they aren't preaching a rodeo," Chance explained.

"Are you preaching a rodeo this week?" Jack asked. For nearly five he and his brother were pretty smart.

She didn't miss the troubled look that shadowed Chance's blue eyes. He shifted uncomfortably as if biding time while he searched for answers. Odd.

She decided to help him out. "Hey, guys, why don't y'all go back outside and play. I'll be out in just a minute. And don't run over any more visitors."

"Okay, Momma," Jack said solemnly. "You want ta come swing with us?" The question was his way of making up to Chance for knocking him down. A child's innocence.

Chance looked surprised and a little pleased. "I'll come watch you before I leave. First I need to talk to your mom."

Jack nodded. "You promise?"

"I promise."

Gavin stopped at the door, holding it open for his twin. "We'll be waitin'. Remember you promised."

Chance smiled at her as they stampeded off but their singsong voices told her how much a promise meant to them.

"You've got good boys," he said the minute the door closed.

"I think so. Rambunctious, but then that's just boys. So, I know you said you weren't preaching right now. But are you doing weddings? I know you did Wyatt and Amanda's. And my friend is really needing a preacher right now."

He shook his head almost too quickly. "No. I'm not doing any pastoral duties right now."

"I guess I didn't think about a pastor taking a vacation," Lynn murmured, not exactly sure how to handle the information. "From what I've heard you're a dedicated man of the Lord. It's just one wedding and it would mean so much to her."

"I'm sorry but I'm taking time off."

He didn't say the words unkindly, but still the man acted as if she'd just asked him to stand in front of an oncoming train. "Maybe if you met Stacy and Emmett. They are—"

"I'm sorry, I really am, but I'm taking time off right now," he said and his tone firmly shut the door on that discussion.

Baffled, she was at a loss for words. The man wasn't thirty yet and he'd been a rodeo pastor for about four years—at least that was what she'd heard someone say down at the diner. And he'd seemed so content when she'd watched him at Wyatt's wedding. Maybe he just needed a rest. Pastors took time off, didn't they? She didn't know what else to say so she just waved a hand toward the lights. "Then, I guess that's a wrap. Thanks for bringing this by. I'll give Melody a call and find out who they're for." She picked up her purse and strode to the door. The man had a right to do what he wanted, but his refusal, without even hearing Stacy's story, irritated her. Really fried her bacon, and that didn't happen often. After all, this was sweet Stacy she was talking about.

"Look, I'm sorry."

She couldn't help hiking a brow at him. "I'm sure you are. Don't let it bother you. I'm sorry my boys accosted you."

"They didn't mean to. I should have been watching out. It was a hard shot to my pride, that's for certain." He held the door for her and she walked past him, more than a little aware of him as she went.

"I can lock up. You go ahead."

He pulled his hat from his head and met her gaze full on. "Is it all right for me to go watch the boys swing for a minute like I promised?"

"Sure." Some of her irritation at him eased as she watched him saunter off in the direction of the boys' shouts of laughter. Chance Turner might not want to pastor right now, but he'd promised her boys he'd watch them swing and he was doing just that.

Such a promise was worth more than most people could even fathom to a pair of boys who'd never had that from their dad.

Lynn didn't want to think about that though. She took a deep breath, walked to the side of the building and watched the looks on their little faces as Chance strode their way. When their eyes lit up she had to fight the lump in her throat and a sudden flood of tears from a past that she had no intention of revisiting.

When the women's shelter in L.A. had burned she'd been thrilled that it had relocated to the sleepy ranching town of Mule Hollow, Texas. Here the cowboys and small-town folks had rallied around them and made a safe haven like nothing she'd ever dreamed of. Her little boys had been too young to remember the life they'd been living before she'd gotten them out. Here in Mule Hollow they had role model after role model of what real men were supposed to be like. Here her sons had the chance to grow up with loving, loyal, honest men and women surrounding them.

What they didn't have was a father. And they wouldn't. Lynn had already come to understand that falling in love wasn't an option she was willing to explore. The safest way to give her boys a good life was to keep it uncomplicated. Besides, she didn't have what it took to cross that line and start looking for love. To love meant to trust and trust wasn't in her anymore. Not trusting with her heart anyway.

But…Chance Turner was intriguing still.

Lynn's heart fluttered as her boys squealed in delight when he said something to them. The flutter just proved that she was still a woman who could appreciate a good-looking, nice man when she saw him. And Chance Turner was a nice man. He'd be nicer if he hadn't refused to perform Stacy's wedding.

Intriguing or not, he was just one more friendly cowboy that her boys could look up to. He was no different than Sheriff Brady Cannon or Deputy Zane Cantrell. Or Dan Dawson or any of the wonderful, Christian men of the community who'd stepped up to be father figures for the kids at the women's shelter.

He spread his legs shoulder-width apart and locked his arms across his chest, watching Gavin and Jack. *Why was he not preaching?* The question niggled at the back of her mind. None of her business though, right?

Right!

"Okay, boys, it's time to hit the road," she called. No use making Chance watch them swing for too long and no reason for her to stand here contemplating issues that had nothing to do with her…except she wished he would consider marrying Stacy and Emmett. *It's none of your business, Lynn*.

"But, Momma—"

"No buts, young man," she said to Gavin. "It's time to head home." She suddenly wanted to grab the boys and hurry away before she opened her mouth and butted in where she shouldn't. The man had a right to preach or not preach. Besides, this was a traditional small-town church. Chance was a rodeo preacher. He moved along with the rodeo circuit, preaching and mentoring the cowboys who couldn't make it to church because of the rodeo's schedule. It was an honorable calling. She liked the idea of what he did…still, while he was here, couldn't he do one wedding?

What could that hurt?

Give it up, Lynn, the man made it clear he was taking time off. Mouth shut, she headed toward her car. She had to bite her tongue again as Chance reached his truck and tipped his hat at her after telling her boys to have a great day.

"Momma, we like him," Jack said the minute he climbed into the seat and buckled his seat belt.

"Yeah," Gavin added, meeting her gaze in the rearview. "Maybe he can teach me how to bull ride."

"There won't be any bull riding for you, mister."

"Aw, Momma. I ain't gonna git myself kilt or anything. Chance ain't dead and neither is Bob or Trace."

Bob Jacobs had been a bull fighter and Trace Crawford had ridden bulls, too. Both men had survived and many other cowboys around town had, too. Still the thought of her little boys growing up to be bull riders didn't sit well with her. "You concentrate on being a little boy and leave the bull riding to the men."

"Aw, Momma, you ain't got to worry. Don'tcha know I'm gonna be the best there ever was."

The hair at the back of her neck prickled but she decided the best thing for now was to let it go. The less said on this subject the better. At least she prayed that was so.

"Well, sugar baby, I think you're the best there ever was already."

"What about me, Momma?" Jack asked.

She turned in her seat. "You know I'm talking about you, too. God must have thought I was pretty special to have blessed me with the two best boys in all of the world."

Chapter Two

"So how are you? Did you get settled into the stage-coach house all right?" Wyatt asked.

Chance hadn't wasted any time getting back to the ranch after his meeting with Lynn Perry and her twins. He'd just climbed into the saddle when Wyatt rode into the yard.

"I'm fine. And yes, I'm settled. How are you? You're looking good. And I'm happy to see you in the saddle again."

Wyatt had insisted on saddling a horse and riding with him. Wyatt sitting in the saddle was a good thing to see, since less than six months ago after his plane crash he'd been relegated to a wheelchair.

Wyatt's lip hitched as he urged his horse forward. "I have the best physical therapist in the world."

Wyatt's wife was his PT. They'd met when she'd come to help him recover. Chance had performed their wedding just a few months earlier and had never expected to be here now. "You don't look like you're doing all right," Wyatt said, shooting Chance one of his penetrating looks. "So don't tell me you're fine. Look, Chance, I know you feel responsible somehow for that bull rider's death but you know as well as I do that it's a profession full of risks."

Perspiration beaded beneath the brim of his hat and his fingers clenched the reins too tightly. Willing himself to relax, Chance studied the flat pasture and welcomed the cold wind on his cheeks and the sting in his eyes. It gave him a barrier to the bitter chill that ran through him each time he thought of Randy. How could he sweat bullets and feel cold to the bone at the same time? *Guilt, that's how.* Gut-wrenching, soul-shredding guilt could make him sick as a dog it tore him up so bad.

"Talk to me, Chance."

"I let him die. Nothing you can say will convince me that I didn't do what I should have done." *I'm just not ready,* had been Randy's last words to Chance before he'd climbed over the rail and settled onto the bull's back. For the last five years Chance had held services every Sunday morning before a rodeo and then he'd stood on the platform with any cowboy who asked. Randy had wanted him there until a few weeks before his death. He'd stopped attending services and avoided him for weeks prior to his last ride. Instead of seeking Randy out, Chance had let other things distract him from going to Randy and showing his concern. Chance knew he was hanging with a rough crowd. He'd known Randy was in danger and yet he hadn't gone the extra mile to try and help him.

"Randy didn't give his life to the Lord. Never accepted the gift of salvation that Jesus offers every person." Wyatt listened intently. "It haunts me." Chance lowered his head for a minute with the weight of the guilt. "I didn't step up when he needed me the most."

"But you were there on his last ride."

He jerked his head up. "Yeah, I was. But he still wasn't ready to commit. I don't know why he asked me that night. It's like he knew in his gut that his time was running out but he couldn't do it. I don't know, Wyatt. I have been over it and over it a thousand times in my mind and I can't figure out what I did wrong. I presented him with every verse and concept about salvation that I could come up with. And I always come up empty…and he always comes up dead. I can't shake knowing that I should have done more. At least stopped him from getting on that bull when I knew he might be doing drugs. It—"

"You can't hold yourself accountable for that."

But he did, and the assortment of prescription drugs that had been found in Randy's gear only made it worse. "I should have stepped in. Rumor had it that it he'd gotten hooked on painkillers after his shoulder injury. His eyes were glazed when I looked at him the moment before the gate opened. And I didn't say anything."

Saying the words was hard for him. Chance knew that logically Randy's death wasn't his fault but that didn't change the way he felt.

"What could you have said? The ride was already in motion. You have to let it go, Chance. I'm telling you it's not your fault." Wyatt's expression was etched with determination. That was Wyatt, always wanting to charge in and save the day. But not this time.

Chance gave a short shake of his head and stared into the distant horizon. He'd messed up. There was no way to wash Randy's blood from his hands. "By omission I let that kid die both physically and spiritually. How am I supposed to live with that?"

"That isn't true," Wyatt snapped, his eyes flashing. "It isn't. You aren't a superhero. The kid was on drugs and he was avoiding you. I get that you hold yourself up to a higher standard, but come on, Chance, let it go."

"I can't, Wyatt. And until I can come to terms with it, there's no way I can stand up in front of a bunch of cowboys or a congregation feeling the way I do. Knowing what I've done."

"Lynn, you need to bid on a bachelor tomorrow night."

Lynn looked up from the centerpiece she was arranging for one of the many tables set up in rows in the community center. Several ladies were scattered about decorating the room for tomorrow night's fundraiser for the women's shelter.

"I'm helping with the benefit, Norma Sue, but I'm not taking part. I've already told you that."

Norma Sue Jenkins hooked her thumb around the strap of her ample overalls, tilted her kinky gray head to the side and grunted, "Hogwash."

"Now, Norma, none of that," Adela Ledbetter-Green admonished in a gentle voice that always made Lynn think of the sugar and spice and everything nice that little girls were made of. God's goodness and grace just radiated from her with a sincerity that made everyone around her feel happier just by being there. It was that loving, sweet spirit that could be misleading to some at times. Because within the elegant, almost fragile-looking form of Adela beat the strong heart of a woman of wisdom, unafraid to speak her mind and give advice and direction whenever she felt the need. Obviously she felt the need, and for that Lynn was grateful.

"Thank you," Lynn said, more than glad to have her support.

Adela smiled and studied her with vibrant peacock-blue eyes. "Well, dear, I didn't say I didn't agree with Norma Sue. I do. I simply think she should be more tempered in her encouragement."

And here Lynn had been thinking all these good thoughts about her!

"Honey, don't look at me so surprised. We just love you to death and want you to be happy."

"I am happy. I just don't want to be pushed." Not even by these ladies she loved so much. And she knew how they could push when they got it in their heads that a woman needed to be matched up and married off. "There will be plenty of women here for y'all to mix and match without me."

"But what about your boys?" Esther Mae Wilcox, their third partner in crime, huffed as she scooted from the table on the other side of Norma Sue. She wore a red velour warm-up suit that clashed totally with her bright, reddish-orange hair. "Don't you think it's time to at least go on *one* date?" At her impatient tone she glanced Adela's way. "Yes, I know I'm pushing when we said we were going to go at this nice and easy. But Adela, I just can't." She hit Lynn with her green eyes. "You were the strongest woman who climbed off that bus two years ago. You have jumped into life here in town with ease and have given your moral support and encouragement to all the other women who have passed through the doors of No Place Like Home. You are always working to help others move forward with their lives and yet you don't."

Lynn couldn't deny any of this. It was true. She'd attended every class at the shelter on overcoming being a battered wife. Every class on coping. Every class under any name, anything that would help her be the woman she needed to be for her boys. She could tell others how to do it and she could help her friends when they needed her. Outwardly she seemed to have her act together and so everyone assumed she did. "Esther Mae, I just moved my boys into their very own home. That's moving forward. I'm happy. I'm content and I'm not bidding on a bachelor."

"Did I hear you say you weren't bidding?" Lacy Brown Matlock asked, coming up behind Lynn. The hugely pregnant hair stylist pulled out a chair beside Lynn and eased down into it. "I'm telling y'all that the doc says this little gal of mine is coming no sooner than two weeks out, but mark my word it'll be sooner rather than later. This baby has a mind of her own and is trying to kick her way out right now!"

Relieved to have someone else join in the conversation, Lynn chuckled. "She's independent like her momma." And they didn't come any more independent than Lacy. She'd moved to Mule Hollow after reading the matchmakers' ad in the newspaper. Just like that, the spunky blonde had followed her heart, determined that if women answered the ad for wives they would not only need their hair and nails done to catch their men, but also they just might need the Lord. Lynn had arrived at the shelter, spirit verging on broken, and gained much inspiration from Lacy. She also knew that Lacy was as much a cupid as the other three ladies.

"*Independent* is the truth," Norma Sue echoed. "I have a feeling Lacy's baby girl is going to hit the ground running."

Esther Mae grinned. "None of us will be able to keep up with the live wire she's destined to be."

"Lacy will," Adela added, reaching across to pat Lacy's arm. "You do look tired though."

She did. Lynn could see fatigue in the high-octane blue of Lacy's eyes. She was glad for the distraction from the subject of Chance, but she wished Lacy didn't look so weary. "Are you sleeping?"

Lacy waved a cherry-pink-tipped hand. "Sleep, what's that? I gave that up weeks ago." She laughed good-naturedly. "Clint says the baby is taking after me with its impetuous nature. We never know when she's going to settle down and when she's not. If I knew, then maybe I'd get some sleep. But when I lay down—at night or even for a little nap—she starts kicking."

"How's Clint holding up?" Lynn liked Clint. The hard-working cattleman sometimes looked at a loss for the things his wife came up with, but there was always a glowing admiration and love in his eyes…even though she'd seen a time or two when he was exasperated. Lacy tended to do that to people though. She got so caught up in what she envisioned for couples that she often acted before thinking things through. Despite that, he loved her…or actually, from what Lynn observed, he loved her because of it. Lynn wouldn't know what that was like. In her marriage she'd learned, slowly, not to voice her opinion, much less make an impulsive move. It had happened over time, practically sneaking up on her. The mental abuse started long before the beatings had occurred.

"Lynn, so you aren't going to bid?"

Lacy's words pelted through the fog of memory like buckshot. "No. I'm not." She braced herself for Lacy to jump on the bandwagon.

"Too bad. I've been praying God would lead the right man to town for you and your boys." Lacy rubbed her extended belly and took a long breath.

"Lacy, you look really tired," Lynn said, concerned.

"Why don't you call it a night?" Norma Sue called out. "You're standing on your feet too much."

Lacy gave a smile—not her normally exuberant one but a smile nonetheless. "You've been talking to Sheri! I sit down when I need to—"

"Ha!" Sheri exclaimed from her perch on a ladder across the room. She cocked her spiky brown head to the side and looked down from where she'd been tacking up red-and-blue bandanna decorations. "You lie, Lacy Matlock! You don't sit down nearly as much as you should. If it were up to me I'd hog-tie you to a couch and make you stay there till our baby comes."

Lacy laughed. "Okay, okay, I get it. I've promised Clint that I'm going to start taking it easy so y'all relax and let me talk to Lynn." Lacy's eyes twinkled like they usually did when she was inspired. "You should bid on Chance. If not for yourself then for him. The man could use some distraction, I think. And you and your sweet boys might just be what the doc upstairs has in mind for him."

Inwardly Lynn groaned as all eyes returned to her. Lacy, the sneak, was trying to turn the tables on her. "I'm not bidding on Chance or anyone else…"

Chance pulled into a parking space in front of Sam's Diner and got out of the truck. There was no way he could come home and not drop by for breakfast at Sam's. His cousins' trucks were lined up along the plank sidewalk and he knew he was running late. Hurrying, he pushed open the diner's heavy swinging door to find Lynn Perry standing on the other side. She was carrying a stack of carryout boxes and coffee in a paper cup. When she saw him she stopped in her tracks.

For a little while the day before, he'd rolled over their meeting in his head, and for the life of him he couldn't stop thinking about her. There was something about her that had edged under his collar and wouldn't let go. She was pretty, with her dark hair and shimmering midnight eyes, but he'd sensed a tough girl underneath her soft image. A tough girl determined to make it for herself and her boys. He liked that.

But she had a keep-your-distance wall erected around her and it was firmly in place right now, even though she was smiling at him.

He tipped his hat and gave her his best smile. "How are you this morning?"

"Great. How are you? I hope you didn't have any lingering aches and pains from yesterday. The boys really didn't mean to lay you out like that."

"I'm fine. Don't worry about me. I've been thrown from horses and bulls that make being taken out by two pint-sized four-year-olds a piece of cake."

She flinched prettily. "It still had to hurt, but I'm glad to see you aren't limping."

"Like I said before, only my pride was hurt."

"Yes, well, that's good—I mean it's good that's all that was hurt."

She sidestepped him to go out the door. "Here, let me," he said, pressing his back to the swinging door and opening it. She edged past him and he got the sweet scent of chocolate as she passed. He couldn't help but lean her way—just his luck, she turned and caught him.

"You, ahhh—" *What?* "You smell good. Is that chocolate?" *Slick, Turner. Way to stick a boot in your mouth.*

She colored rose-pink and he could tell he'd flustered her. He'd flustered himself! He could flirt with the best of them but it had been a while since he'd done it. He was about as rusty as a bucket of wet nails.

"I've been mixing chocolate bars since seven."

"Sweet. I mean, sweet job."

He figured she was probably ready to toss her coffee on him but she chuckled instead and walked off without another word. She probably thought he was a lost cause. Come to think of it, maybe he was. He watched her cross the street and push open the door to the candy store.

"You jest gonna stand thar and stare all day or ya gonna come in and have a bite to eat?"

He should have known Applegate Thornton would be sitting at his usual seat by the window. The old coot's booming voice probably could be heard across the street at the candy store. But at least it had Chance moving back inside and not standing halfway out on the sidewalk.

Ignoring the laughter from the table in the center of the room where his cousins were sitting, he strode to the window table to see App and his buddy Stanley Orr. "It's good to see you two are still holding down the fort. How's it going?"

Applegate grinned. "We ain't doin' nearly as good as you, son. Lynn was lookin' mighty sweet at you. Stanley, you ever seen Lynn lookin' at anybody like that?"

Stanley was slightly balding, plump and about the easiest-going man Chance had ever been around. "Nope, can't say I have. You got a ticket to the steak dinner tomorrow night?"

"Yes, he has a ticket," Cole called from the table where he, Wyatt and Seth were watching Chance like hawks.

"I didn't buy a ticket."

"The ranch bought it for you," Seth said.

He took the fourth cane-backed chair at the table and sank into it. "I don't remember saying I wanted to attend a steak dinner."

"It's for a good cause," Seth said, taking a drink of his coffee, just as Sam, the owner of the diner, came striding toward their table with coffeepot in hand.

Small and wiry, with a quick step, Sam gave a hearty smile. "It's good ta see ya, son!" He set a coffee mug in front of Chance then shook his hand fiercely. "I was sure sorry ta hear about that bull rider. A cry'n shame is what that was." Shaking his head he poured coffee into the mug.

Chance wrapped his hands around the warm cup and

felt the stab of deep regret. "Yeah, it was." All eyes were on him right now. He didn't want to discuss this.

"All you could be was there fer them if they needed you."

Chance met Sam's wise, gray eyes. How could he say that he hadn't been there for Randy? That in his heart of hearts he felt—

"Yor taken his death pretty hard, ain't ya?"

"Yes, he is," Cole answered for him.

Chance met his gaze across the table. His cousin had been running hard from his past for years after his fiancée's death. He was settled and happy now, thanks to a beautiful country vet named Susan. Cole was more content than he'd ever been and he and Susan were planning on starting a family soon. He'd been through a lot and found solace in helping disaster victims rebuild their homes during the time that he lost his way. Chance stared into the black coffee and wondered if that was what he'd done…lost his way. Ever since that horrible night he just couldn't think of himself as a pastor. It ate at him.

"That's what makes you good at what you do, Chance," Cole continued. "You care. You can't be a pastor, a shepherd to your sheep, and not care."

He felt as far away from being a shepherd as he could possibly get. Talk about a gulf…

"So don't keep beating yourself up with things that were out of your control," Seth, the control freak of the Turners, added. Chance looked at him in disbelief. Seth grinned. "Yeah, you heard right. That coming from me. I've been learning to let God handle things more. Not that it's been a bed of roses. Old habits are hard to break. But I'm working on it."

Chance had been handing out advice right and left, thinking he was making sense. Funny how it all seemed out of focus to him right now. "Can we talk about something else?" He didn't want to be rude but he felt like he was swinging zeros.

Sam squeezed his shoulder. "You were reckless but you always was one to take the world on yor shoulders. You got a big heart, Chance, even after all you went through. I gotta git back ta work, but you listen ta these boys and pull yourself out of this spot yor in. My eggs and bacon'll help ya. That all right by y'all?"

Everyone gave hearty agreement and Sam strode off on his bowlegs. Chance knew Sam had been referring to Chance's childhood...he'd long ago come to terms with the fact that his dad had had better things to do than raise his son. Chance had been hard to deal with at an early age and his mother hadn't known what to do with him. He'd spent many summers here in Mule Hollow with his cousins. Their dad had loved him and treated him like his own, worked him hard and given him as much direction and love as he gave his own sons. But in his early teens Chance had rebelled against his dad's lack of interest and he'd hit the road...it had been a hard time. Too heavy for him to think about right now.

"Look, Chance, take it from my experience." Seth glanced around the table at his brothers. "God is in control even when we don't understand or don't agree. You've given us all that advice at some point in time."

"Yeah, I was pretty liberal handing it out, wasn't I?"

He grunted, his mood taking a downhill turn and picking up speed.

Wyatt frowned. "You hand out great advice. I owe you and there's no two ways about it. God sent you to me with the advice I needed to hear just when I needed to hear it. I was about as low as a man can get and you helped me see what I needed to do to help Amanda. You just have to heed your own good advice and give this over to the Lord. We've all been where you're at, and it's not a fun place to be."

Applegate and Stanley had been pretending like they were engrossed in their morning checkers game—why they were even pretending was a mystery to Chance. For two men who couldn't hear they heard everything. It was a miracle beyond understanding, which made Chance smile—some much-needed relief from the downturn of this conversation. App spat a sunflower seed into the brass spittoon at his feet and Stanley did the same. Both hit the opening in the conversation dead-on.

"Sounds ta me like that steak dinner is jest the place you need ta be. Don't you thank so, Stanley?"

"Yup. Ain't nothin' like a good steak and the company of pretty women ta pull a man out of the dumps."

"A woman is the last thing I need to be thinking about."

"It ain't us that caused Lynn ta blush," App grunted. "You got a free ticket and a woebegone attitude that needs sprucing up. Put on some starched jeans and a crisp shirt, slap on a little smell-good and join the festivities."

Sam came out of the kitchen loaded down with plates. Chance had never been so glad to see a plate of eggs in all his life. Maybe putting food in their stomachs would get them off him.

"And speaking of other thangs," App drawled, his lean face cascading into a dour look. "We need a preacher. No two ways about it. I been thankin' that thar is the reason the good Lord brought you home." App had made it clear at Wyatt's wedding that he thought Chance should come home to Mule Hollow and become the pastor of the church. Chance had told him then that he didn't feel called to preach in a local church. That should have ended the discussion, but App wasn't known for letting go of things and it looked like he hadn't let this go either. "So what do ya say?"

Chance looked at the steaming breakfast plate and took a long, slow breath. So much for thinking the food was going to get him off the hot seat.

Chapter Three

The morning after Chance had flustered her by telling her she smelled sweet, Lynn *dreamed* about him! Oh yeah, but thankfully she was awakened from dreaming about the hunky, dark-haired bachelor by her horse of a dog, Tiny. Her unlikely hero bounded onto her bed and pounced on her with all four of his huge paws! The power of the attack knocked the wind *and* the dream right out of her.

"Thank you," she gasped, trying to get her breath back as she stared into Tiny's pale face. His excited are-you-ready-to-play eyes danced as he gaped at her. She relaxed, relieved to be awake…it wasn't unusual for her to have nightmares. Though they had slowly become less frequent and they were always about her ex-husband… Dreaming about Chance Turner was disturbing on an entirely different level. Thank goodness for Tiny.

"What are you doing in the house?" she asked, making certain not to scold. The boys sometimes tried to sneak the giant animal into the house, or when they went outside they forgot to close the door and Tiny would sneak into the house by himself. On those occasions there was never any telling what he was going to get into. And if you scolded him he tended to leave puddles—and that wasn't a good thing.

The sound of erratic hammering filled the air outside her window. She glanced at the bedside clock—seven o'clock. Tiny danced on top of her, tail wagging, breath huffing, eyes twinkling, he barked excitedly and looked toward the window.

"Okay, okay. I get it." Gently pushing the oversize pup off her, she padded to the window and pulled aside the curtain.

Before going to help decorate for the auction—and getting attacked by her friends—she had worked a full day at the candy store. Her boys had spent the day at Amanda Turner's place. Amanda couldn't have children of her own and since marrying Chance's cousin, Wyatt, she often enjoyed having Gavin and Jack over to play when Lynn needed a babysitter. She and Wyatt were in the process of trying to adopt, and there was no doubt in anyone's mind that any baby would be blessed to have her and Wyatt as parents.

Just after Lynn had told everyone that she was not bidding on a bachelor, Amanda and her two sisters-in-law, Susan and Melody, had arrived with the kids.

Melody had asked about the lights and the boys had immediately told everyone about how they'd caused Chance to fall and dump the lights all over himself. Everyone got a good laugh and she'd seen the spark of excitement burn brighter in the three matchmaking buddies' mischievous eyes. That was all it had taken for them to be off and running with stories about Chance when he was growing up—Chance Turner had been a handful. Of course, her boys had jumped right into the fray, giggling at stories of the things Chance and his cousins had gotten into.

She had also been informed by Melody that the Christmas lights he'd brought up to the church were for her, and that they were to be used to decorate her new house. Lynn had been touched by the gift and told Melody so. All their questions about Chance and what she thought of him had taken her by surprise and left her suspicious. Mule Hollow was known for its matchmaking, after all.

She and the boys had been late getting home and they'd all been tired. The last thing she expected to see when she looked out the window this morning was Gavin and Jack outside attacking the large oak tree in the backyard with hammers.

"What are they doing?" she asked, looking down at Tiny.

The dog placed his paws on the windowsill and whined as he studied them. His tail wagged impatiently, signaling that he wanted to be out there with his boys. "Come on, let's go." That was all it took. The dog shot out of her bedroom like a flash. Lynn grabbed her housecoat off the bed as she passed. It was chilly in the house and she stopped to turn the thermostat up a notch or two. She put on her leather slides beside the back door, which was cracked open but not enough for the dog to escape. Lynn guessed that he'd snuck inside when the boys left it ajar and then the draft must have sucked it shut, trapping him.

Tiny wiggled with anticipation and the instant she pulled the door open he shot outside and was gone. Lynn agreed with him—life was never dull with Gavin and Jack around. She trailed him.

Jack had both hands wrapped around the middle of a hammer that was as long as his arm. Gavin held a twelve-inch piece of old barn wood against the tree. Both of them looked up at her as she approached. Tiny stuck his nose into the mix and Gavin pushed it away.

"What are you two little mischief makers doing?"

"Workin', Mom," Jack answered, slamming the head of the hammer at the nail protruding at an angle from the piece of wood. He missed.

"We're gonna build a tree house." Gavin nodded toward the old shed at the back of the yard. "There's a whole bunch of wood in there we can use." His high-pitched voice was shrill with excitement.

Jack again whacked the nail, which bent over and smashed against the wood. She cringed—better the wood than his finger. His shoulders slumped and his face fell as he let the hammer drop to his side. He looked so dejected it was all Lynn could do not to scoop him up and hug him tight.

Gavin scrunched his brows together looking at him. "That's okay, Jack. I didn't do no better."

Her little men, her heart tugged. "Building a tree house sounds like a great plan, guys. But let's put the hammer up for now. It's time to get ready for church. When we get home I'll come out here and we'll take a look at what's in the shed and see what we can do." Like she could actually build something! Who was she kidding?

"But you're a girl, Momma."

Oh, the challenge of it. "Yes, Jack, I am. But girls can

build tree houses, too." She was sure some girls could. Whether or not *she* could was yet to be seen.

"You sure?" Gavin asked, looking as skeptical as she felt.

"Yes, Gavin, I am. Now come inside and let's get dressed for church."

"Momma, I bet Chance can build a tree house."

Not again. Her boys had been around Chance for only a short time and for some reason they were fascinated by everything about the man. "Gavin, I've already told you he's Mr. Turner to both of you. And he probably is very good at building things," she admitted as she opened the door for them. "Wipe your boots off." They made extravagant swipes of their boots on the rug and then hurried off to their rooms. Tiny tried to follow but Lynn grabbed him. "Oh, no you don't, buster." She pulled him outside, patted his head and then firmly closed the door.

She walked to the sink and stared out the window at the tree with the board attached and the hammers leaning against it. Chance probably could build a tree house her boys would be proud of. The man looked like he could do anything. There was just something about him that gave off that vibe. She felt it, and that had to be what her boys were sensing even though they were too young to realize it.

"Mom! Jack won't give me my shirt," Gavin yelled from the back room.

"It's my shirt," Jack yelled back.

She closed her eyes and shook her head. Her boys got along for the most part, but brothers would be brothers... Pushing thoughts of Chance from her mind she went to see what was going on. She was so happy to have the small house of her own that even the sounds of her boys fussing made the place seem homey. It was wonderful to know that she was providing a roof over her sons' heads in this peaceful ranching community.

The other women who had arrived with her in the van from L.A. were also moving on with their lives, slowly but surely, just like Esther Mae had said. Lynn had helped many of them in some way. Rose, the only mother with a teenage son, had been the first to move out of the shelter and had married not too long after that. Nive was still at the shelter, and so was Stacy, who was about to get married. All of them had come a long way since arriving here in Mule Hollow. And there were others after them who came, too. Some had used the facility as a temporary stopping point before finding a permanent shelter elsewhere, but for the original four Mule Hollow was now home. It was a great place to raise boys. The country life suited them and it suited Lynn, too.

"It's mine—"

"No. It's mine—"

She found them having a tug-of-war over a blue shirt. "Guys, what's going on here?"

"It's my shirt," Jack said.

Gavin shook his head. "It's mine."

Lynn looked at the shirt. "You both have this same exact shirt… Let's take a look at them." Getting dressed for church was not always an easy process. Raising boys was challenging, but she wouldn't give it up for anything. Sometimes, though, she worried about the future and not having a man in their lives to help guide the boys.

Should she start looking for a man to fill the blank spot their dad had left? The thought hit her at times like this. When things like the tree house cropped up. It made her feel guilty that she wasn't ready.

The ladies pressuring her about the bachelor auction didn't help either. They didn't understand—how could they know how she felt when she'd never told them? All her life she'd lived in turmoil where men were concerned—until now.

No one knew exactly how bad her life had been prior to escaping to the shelter. She wanted it to stay that way, too. Hiding her emotions had worn her down, but for the first time in years she was living life contentedly.

With no man in the picture there was no danger. No broken trust, no risk of being hurt…it was easier. Safer.

Both physically and emotionally. It had taken the love and fear for her sons to drive her from the cycle of abuse. Knowing that if not for them she might still be there undermined her self-respect and scared her.

No. It was better this way. Better feeling strong and content that her boys were her life. They were safe and happy as they were. And no matter how guilty she might feel because they didn't have a father in their lives, she wasn't ready to change that, not even for them.

Church had started when Chance slid into the back pew. He felt awkward arriving late but he hadn't planned on coming at all. At the last minute the Lord, or habit, had him heading to the church. Normally his church was a dusty or waterlogged arena prior to a competition's start.

Miss Adela had been playing the piano for the Mule Hollow Church of Faith all of Chance's life. She had just finished playing the welcoming hymn "When We All Get to Heaven" as he slipped into the pew beside Applegate.

"This back pew's not the place fer you, Chance Turner," App leaned in and whispered loudly.

So much for thinking he'd gotten his point across yesterday. "Good morning to you, too, App."

Applegate hiked a bushy brow. "What's good about it? We're at church and the only preacher we've got is sittin' in the back row with me."

Several people turned at his words. Since App was hard of hearing and talked loud enough to be heard in the choir loft it was a wonder the entire congregation didn't turn and look at him. Well, okay, so most of them did. Chance had known this would happen but here he was anyway. It was like the Lord wasn't going to let him go even when He knew Chance was struggling. "App, sir," he whispered, "now isn't the time for me to be up there."

App crossed his arms and grunted just as Brady Cannon stepped up to the podium. The sheriff taught the singles' Sunday school class, and he and his wife, Dottie, had turned his ranch into a shelter for abused women. Chance respected them both very much. Dottie ran a candy store on Main Street where she taught the women how to run their own business. Being self-sufficient was a goal of the shelter along with helping the families overcome their abusive pasts.

Wyatt had told him that Lynn, the woman he'd met yesterday, had recently moved from the shelter into her own place with her two sons. He wondered about Lynn. He'd hated to hear she'd had a hard time in her life. How a man could hurt a woman was beyond him…but how he could vow before God to love and cherish her and then strike and abuse her was even more incomprehensible.

"As most of you know I'm a sheriff, not a preacher," Brady began to speak. "I'm just the best you've got this morning. Or at least that's what the elders tell me. I'm pretty certain there's some of you out there who could do a much better job than me of preaching this morning. I hope whoever you are that you'll step up and fill the need."

App shot Chance a sharp look, and he felt eyes on him from everywhere else, too. Looking to the right he saw two small heads, one dark and one blond, turned his way. Gavin and Jack were barely able to see him over the back of the pew but they were watching him. Their mother sat beside them with her gaze focused straight ahead on Brady. When the boys saw Chance looking, the blonde raised his hand and waved. The dark-headed one followed suit. Lynn caught their movement out of the corner of her eye and automatically turned. Her midnight eyes locked with Chance's and unexpectedly his mouth went dry and his pulse tripped all over itself, pounding erratically.

Something in that look hadn't been there before. Something in the way her eyes blazed into his hadn't seared into him like that yesterday. The moment lasted less than a second before she let her gaze drop to her boys, tapping them each on the head and telling them, with the swirl of her finger, to turn around. Less than a second but he was hung up…

App elbowed him. "Like I said yesterday, she don't look at jest anybody like that. If you was in the pulpit you wouldn't have ta be lookin' at the back of her pretty head right now."

The woman in front of him almost choked on her laughter as she tried to hide that she'd heard what App had said. Why hide it? Everyone would have heard him, but they were all listening intently to Brady. Chance knew there was no way they hadn't heard App, but they were doing a good job not disturbing the service any more than it already had been.

"App, cut it out," he growled.

Thankfully, App decided he'd said enough. He crossed his arms and stared straight ahead for the remainder of Brady's lesson.

The sheriff did a good job over the next twenty minutes. His words were about being a good steward of the talents God had given each church member, something Chance had thought he was doing until Randy's death.

Though Chance listened, his heart was closed off to any emotional response. It had been that way ever since Randy had fallen beneath the hooves of that bull and Chance had realized he probably wasn't coming out alive. App could push all he wanted but Chance wasn't up to being in that pulpit right now. And honestly, he wasn't sure when or if he'd be ready. He felt as if a heavy horse blanket had been thrown around his heart, smothering out all the light.

Everyone kept saying he needed time. That was why he'd come home. Time could heal most everything.

Chance hoped it was true.

He'd given many a cowboy a similar sermon at different times of trial in their lives. Now he was seeing how much easier it was to spout the words when you were giving advice to someone else. It was different when you were the one in the midst of the storm.

He let his gaze slide toward Lynn once more. Something was bothering her, too. He saw it in her eyes just now, and it cut him to the core.

Chapter Four

"**H**ey, mister. Mr. Chance, hold up."

"Yeah, hold up!"

Chance had cut out the second the prayer was over. He wanted to keep right on walking but no way could he ignore the small voices hailing him. He'd made straight for the parking lot and was almost to the edge of the grass, almost to the white rock and fifteen feet from his truck... He'd almost made it.

App's grumbling during the sermon had convinced Chance that if he hung around he'd never hear the end of it. But no way could he ignore Gavin and Jack.

Feeling roped and tied he turned on his heel to find both boys charging after him. Lynn followed at a slow, reluctant pace. And he groaned at the sight of the Mule Hollow posse behind her! Norma Sue Jenkins and Esther Mae Wilcox were two of the older ladies who kept Mule Hollow running smoothly. They, along with their buddy Adela, had saved the tiny town with their matchmaking antics.

They'd come up with the idea a couple of years earlier to advertise for wives for all the lonesome cowboys who lived and worked the ranching area. Despite the disbelief of everyone around them, lo and behold, women read the ads and had begun to come to town. Since then the ladies were always coming up with special events that would draw women to the town. Like dinner theater with the cowboys singing and serving, or festivals where the cowboys and ladies would meet up. So far it had worked well. He appreciated the three women, but they were also among the ones who were adamant about him coming home to preach.

Watching their approach he prepared himself for a lecture.

"Boys," Lynn called, coming to a halt behind the two little dudes.

He couldn't help but wonder what was bothering her so…why she looked pensive and almost frightened. Was she scared of him?

"Mr. Turner was leaving. You don't need to bother him."

"We ain't, Momma." Gavin batted big eyes at her and then at him. "We was just wonderin' if you know how to make a tree house?"

"Yeah," Jack drew the word out dismally as he wagged his dark head back and forth. "We got a *mess* at our house. A pure mess."

"Boys!" Lynn exclaimed, turning red as a poinsettia, her big dark eyes widening like she'd just been prodded with an electric cattle prod.

Esther Mae and Norma Sue came to a halt, catching the end of Jack's declaration. Chance had a feeling Lynn was just as reluctant in their presence as he was. Matchmakers. Scary stuff for people who wanted nothing to do with the subject.

"Y'all are building a tree house—how fun!" Esther Mae exclaimed. Her red hair almost matched the color on Lynn's cheeks as they flamed up even brighter.

"We—well, the boys—started one this morning."

"That's a wonderful idea," Norma Sue boomed. "You boys probably do need a man to help you get that tree house up and working."

Chance didn't miss the flash of alarm in Lynn's eyes when Norma Sue spoke. He understood. He didn't know what to say. He didn't want to build a tree house. He wanted to be alone right now. To go back out to the stagecoach house where he was staying to contemplate the state of his life. Alone. And he could see that was what she wanted, too.

But Jack and Gavin were looking up at him with adoring eyes! *Adoring*—what exactly had he done to deserve the look in those eyes?

He met Lynn's now fiery gaze and his mouth went dry for the second time that day. She was struggling to hold her temper. It was obvious she didn't want his help. He told himself this had to do with her background. This was wariness or maybe distrust that he was feeling from her. He didn't like what he saw in the depths of her eyes and his own hackles went up at the idea she'd been mistreated. How bad had her abuse been? The question dug in like spurs.

"I could help if you need me." What else could he say? The boys yelled jubilantly and began jumping around with happiness.

Lynn pressed her shoulders back and shook her head.

"Thank you," she said, stiffly, "but we don't need help building our tree house."

"I don't mind." *Chance, what are you saying?*

"He don't mind, Momma."

"Gavin, you're showing very bad manners. Again, thank you but we're fine," she said firmly. "Come on, boys, we need to go."

"But, Momma—"

"Jack, we need to go home. Remember we have Christmas lights to put up, too."

Both boys looked reluctantly at him but obediently headed off to the car. Lynn didn't meet his gaze as she said goodbye to Norma Sue and Esther Mae. He thought she was just going to walk off but then she paused. "I'm sorry. Thanks for the offer though," she said, then strode away.

What had she been through?

Chance's cousins walked up. "What was that all about?" Wyatt asked.

"That was Lynn being stubborn," Norma Sue offered. "Gavin and Jack were trying to get Chance to help them build a tree house, but Lynn is Miss Independent and having none of that."

Esther Mae harrumphed. "She needs to get over that."

Wyatt got a thoughtful gleam in his eye. *"Really."*

Cole grinned. He was the youngest brother, about Chance's age and his former partner in crime. "Did you tell them you were a master tree house builder?"

"I think we can both swing a hammer better than we could back then." Chance chuckled. He and Cole had tried to build a tree house when they were about eight years old. "We were stubborn back then though. We refused help from everyone."

"Until Dad stepped in," Wyatt added. "Y'all had the biggest mess. Dad finally had to insist on making it safe for y'all to use."

"Thank goodness." Seth gave a laugh that was more of a grunt. "Oh, by the way, I forgot to tell you Melody said thanks for taking those lights up to the church for her."

Esther Mae beamed. "Lynn told us about that last night when we were decorating for the fundraiser. What a cute way to meet," she gushed. "Are you coming to the fundraiser tonight?"

Chance had already told Wyatt and all the guys the day before that he was going to pass. Wyatt hadn't liked it and had told him that being around people would be good for him, but he understood. Now, looking at Esther Mae and Norma Sue, Chance wasn't sure what to say. They had worked hard on this fundraiser, evidently, and it was for a good cause. His conscience pricked at him. He was startled that they hadn't yet mentioned his preaching. He was relieved by the reprieve. "I'm not sure—"

"Sure you are." Norma Sue looked serious. "Chance, we just heard what a hard time you're having dealing with the loss of this young man. The best thing is for you to get involved with your family…and we are your family. I expect to see you there." She shot Wyatt a firm look. "See to it."

Wyatt gave a slow grin. "Yes, ma'am. You heard the lady, Chance."

He was dug in deep for patience.

Esther Mae dipped her chin, causing the yellow daffodils on her hat to bend forward as if they, too, were watching Chance. "I'm expecting you there, too. So don't disappoint me. I know you'll enjoy it. And it will be good for you. Lynn will be there, too."

Great, just what he needed. Chance wondered what Lynn would think if she knew what was going on.

"And you'll enjoy the auction, too," Cole drawled.

"What auction? I haven't heard anything about that."

Seth hiked a shoulder. "Aw, it's just stuff for the ladies."

"But you'll still enjoy seeing them bid," Norma Sue added quickly, and Esther Mae grinned and nodded.

Everyone was acting strange. He knew they cared for him and maybe they were right. "I might be there," he offered.

Chance thought about Norma Sue's words all the way back to the stagecoach house. As he drove down the gravel road to the house that had been in the Turner family for almost two hundred years, he felt a small semblance of peace. His home was basically on the road, but when he needed time out this was where he came—always had been. All the memories he had from his years spent visiting and living at the ranch were the good times. Yes, he'd come home for much-needed solitude and time to think. But as he pulled up in front of the stagecoach house and got out of the truck he knew at six o'clock he'd be getting back in the truck and heading back to town.

This was a fundraiser...and the least he could do was go up there and buy a steak to help raise money for the women's shelter. There was no denying the good the shelter did. It was evident in Lynn and her boys. He'd spend some time alone tomorrow, but he knew he wouldn't feel good about himself if he didn't go up there and make a contribution to the shelter. Many benefits had been held to help Randy's family after his death. He'd only made it to one of them and he'd been asked to speak. He'd almost not made it through that… No, helping out the shelter here at home was the least he could do.

The women must really like whatever was up for bids. They were everywhere.

Chance walked through the door of the community center, which was just down the sidewalk past Pete's Feed and Seed. He'd had to park all the way at the opposite end past Sam's Diner just to find a parking space.

There were lots of couples sitting around and mingling in groups, but it was immediately obvious that the room was overrun by single women. He should have known that any gathering the town was organizing would bring even more women to Mule Hollow to meet single cowboys. His cousins had expanded their cattle operation, as had several other large ranches in the area, increasing the cowboy population even more. All in all, Mule Hollow had grown in the last year, and by the crowd it was apparent.

Glancing around, Chance had thought maybe he'd see a bunch of beauty-treatment baskets or jewelry or stuff that ladies liked, lining a table somewhere to be auctioned off. But he didn't see anything like that.

"Chance, over here," Wyatt called, waving him over

to join the family. He wove his way through the tables, greeting people as he went.

"Boy, you weren't kidding when you said the women were going to bid. What's up for bids?" he asked, taking a seat beside Wyatt. There were two women at the table in front of him giving him the once-over... He felt like *he* was the one on the auction block.

Wyatt's wife, Amanda, gaped at him like he was crazy. "You don't know?"

"Know what?" He glanced around the table. Seth, Cole and Wyatt had on poker faces that would have made their great, great, great, great, great Grandpa Oakley proud. Oakley wasn't the most respectable Turner in the clan and immediately Chance was on alert. Melody, Amanda and Susan's expressions of disbelief sent an uneasy feeling coursing through his veins. "What have I missed?"

Amanda pushed her short dark hair behind her ear. "I can't believe no one told you?" She gave Wyatt a cute scowl. "Or that you didn't see the flyers on the fronts of the stores announcing that this is a dinner and bachelor auction."

Chance choked. "A what? What flyers? You said a *bachelor auction?*" He cut his gaze to Wyatt, then Cole and Seth, and he was pretty certain his scowl wasn't cute. He hadn't been in town all that much, but now that he thought about it he had seen a flash of yellow on the windows. Suddenly he remembered seeing Sam crumbling up something yellow when he was getting out of the truck for breakfast the day before. He'd also been grinning when he greeted Chance at the door. "What exactly are y'all up to?" he asked, knowing he'd been set up.

"It's harmless," Susan said, shooting Cole a disbelieving glance. "The women or anyone who wants to can bid on the bachelors who have agreed to be auctioned off. The high bidders have to fix dinner for the cowboy they win and then he gives them a few hours of work around their house."

Melody leaned around Seth and smiled sweetly. "You know, like help with putting up their *Christmas lights*," she said, drawing out the obvious. "Or cleaning up their yard to get ready for the holidays."

Had that had been why she'd given all those lights to Lynn? Was Melody expecting Lynn to bid on a bachelor? As if summoned by his thoughts he spotted Lynn across the room dishing salad onto plates. He noticed the waiters then, about fifteen cowboys carrying plates to the tables.

"Are those the cowboys who agreed to be auctioned?" he asked Wyatt.

"Yup, that's them."

"You know cowboys," Cole drawled. "They'll sacrifice themselves for a good cause."

Yeah, right. *Big sacrifice.* Judging by the grins on their faces they weren't hurting too bad. Chance massaged the knot that had formed in his neck. It was no coincidence that everyone had conveniently omitted that this was a bachelor auction. Why?

Across the room he caught sight of Lynn. She was busy, in and out of the kitchen with several other women and men. Applegate and Stanley were manning the grill out back, so he'd been told. Every once in a while he saw them carry in pans of steaks. Lynn was putting food on plates. She looked as pretty as a summer day wearing a yellow sweater with her jeans. She caught him staring at her several times—he'd make an effort to stop staring but next thing he knew, he was right back at it. It was nothing short of rude, so why was he doing it?

Feeling eyes on him, he glanced around and caught Brady watching him from the next table. The sheriff leaned toward Chance across the space between the tables so he could speak quietly to him.

"It was good to see you in church Sunday. You were far more qualified than me to be in that pulpit though."

"You did a great job."

Brady rested his elbow on his thigh. "Don't know about that, but seriously—I know your heart is at the arena with the cowboys, but we could really use you while you're in town. With Christmas coming and no preacher in sight…I mean, to be honest, we haven't gotten any replies to our request. I can only do so much because I'm not a preacher. I have faith that God's going to send the right man for the job, but I'm not sure when that will be."

Chance really admired Brady for what he was doing. If there was ever a born leader Brady was it. Not only was he a big man physically but he was a man of big integrity, too. He deserved an honest, open answer. Chance leaned closer so their conversation couldn't be overheard. "Look, Brady, I've got to sort out some personal issues right now before I could stand up there in front of the church. My heart has to be clear and since Randy died—"

"That's the bull rider that got killed a few weeks ago?"

"Yeah, that's him. I'd been witnessing to him for some time. He'd gotten mixed up in some bad stuff but all I needed was a little more time. I know he'd have accepted the Lord…with just a little more time. I don't know why God didn't allow that."

Brady hung his head then, met his gaze with regret in his eyes. "I guess preachers are human too, aren't you? We can look at a preacher and expect you never to have a crisis or any anger…but it happens."

Anger. It was true he was angry. And he was in a crisis of faith. Brady had him pegged. But then, he was a sheriff with skill in reading situations. "Yeah, it happens. I'm sorry. I'd like to help out, but even though I'm out of sorts right now I still have confidence that God's going to send the right man to Mule Hollow."

Brady nodded. "You're right. I'll just keep plugging away best I can. I'll also pray He'll help sort out things for you." He started to sit up straight and let Chance get back to his table but halted halfway and leaned back toward him, speaking quietly again for only Chance's ears. "Lynn over there is a great gal. She's sorting through her own issues at her own pace. Dottie and I are praying God sends the right man into her life when the time is right. She deserves it."

Chance wasn't sure if he was getting a warning but he nodded. "She seems like a good person."

"She is. All these women are, in the shelter. They've had it rough but they're fighters. Lynn's their advocate in many ways, pushing them to heal and move forward with their lives, but…" He paused as steaks were brought to his table. "I'm talking too much. It's time to eat, then I have an auction to get underway. You think about what I said. If you need to talk, come by my office."

"I'll do that." Chance glanced up and saw Lynn making her way toward him. She took the empty seat at Brady's table directly across from him, and as she sat down she caught Chance watching her. Again. She gave him a tentative smile, then began talking to a pretty blonde whose gaze was riveted on one of the cowboys—a nervous fella who was barely getting his job done for looking back at her.

"Who is that lady sitting beside Lynn?" he asked Wyatt.

"That's Stacy. She and Emmett are planning on getting married—*if* she ever decides on who is going to perform the ceremony. And if you haven't figured out who Emmett is, he's the cowboy who keeps bumping into tables because he can't function without looking at Stacy."

It was pretty obvious who Emmett was. The red-faced cowboy was going to dump a steak on somebody if he didn't watch out where he was going. Chance remembered Lynn asking if he performed weddings. "So, if they're getting married why is he one of the waiters? Didn't you say the waiters were the ones getting auctioned?"

"They needed more men and since he's a nice guy who is grateful the shelter brought Stacy into his life, he offered to fill in."

"I see," he said, but really he didn't. He sliced a piece of his steak. It was tender and, like all the steaks at a shindig like this, cooked medium to save on confusion and time. He watched the cowboys pass out the last plates, flirting with the ladies as they served. "From the looks of things the shelter might make a pretty penny." His gaze slid toward Lynn. She was watching him, though she looked away quickly and concentrated on her own meal the moment their eyes met.

"Hey, cousin, we want to auction you off." Cole cocked a brow.

"That's the plan," Wyatt agreed, and the rest of the table nodded enthusiastically.

"Oh, no, you don't." Chance got all hot under the collar looking at them—his ears were hot, he was so tense. "I told y'all not to go gettin' any ideas," he warned, glancing across at Lynn and seeing a pink stain on her cheeks. Though she wasn't looking at him, he got the feeling she'd heard everything.

Wyatt shot him one of his piercing looks and Chance could see the wheels in his lawyer's head chugging away. This wasn't good. When Wyatt got an idea about something there wasn't much to stop him. Even so, Chance tried. "Wyatt, don't even think about it." Could they not see that she didn't want any of this?

"I was just thinking about those little boys this morning wanting you to help them with their tree house. It would be nice to help them out."

Chance saw Lynn stiffen and her sharp gaze met his briefly before she looked away—no doubt about whether or not she'd heard that. "She didn't want my help," he said, his voice low to keep it from carrying. "She made that clear." He looked at Wyatt with real warning in his eyes. It was then that he noticed how quiet the table had grown, and his attention was drawn around to the bright, well-intentioned eyes of his family. Not one of them was paying his warning any attention.

His gaze slid back to Lynn. Randy hadn't wanted his help either, and Chance had failed him because he hadn't pursued helping him anyway. But this wasn't the same.

Not the same at all.

Chapter Five

"Who'll give me one-fifty for Emmett? He's a hard worker, *and*..." Brady paused to grin at the roomful of people before zeroing in on Stacy, who blushed profusely when all eyes turned to her. "From what I hear he's a good cook, too. A bit on the shy side so you might have a hard time getting any talk out of him." A round of laughter erupted from across the room. Red-faced, Emmett stood beside Brady. When a lively round of bidding instantly ensued he looked even more embarrassed. Lynn's heart went out to the lanky, quiet cowboy. The poor guy was not the most handsome cowboy in the room—some might even say he was homely because he was so thin and red-faced. But within his skinny chest there was a loyal heart of gold. A humble man of honor, he'd given his heart to only one lucky woman in the room. He'd fallen in love with Stacy the day she stepped off the van that had brought Lynn and the others to No Place Like Home. God truly had worked in mysterious ways to get them here, and she was forever grateful.

Stacy had been through so much, having grown up with an abusive father, then continuing the cycle by marrying an abusive man. The shelter had saved her and when they'd moved to Mule Hollow, Emmett had patiently, sweetly been there for her over the last two years as she healed emotionally. Both he and Stacy were quiet, and it had taken a year to get them to actually talk more than a few sentences to each other. It had been a touching thing to watch. Lynn knew she'd been a part of helping Stacy let go of some of the pain from her past and reach out for the bright future she could have with Emmett. Knowing this gave Lynn great satisfaction.

When the bidding finally eased up after going another hundred dollars higher, Emmett shifted and looked pained. The bidding had slowed now but he seemed ready to bolt. He'd known when he entered the auction that Stacy wouldn't have a lot of money to bid on him and he'd thought that was okay because he didn't figure there would be much bidding going on for him anyway. Still, he'd confided that he was worried about the situation. He hadn't counted on Norma Sue and Esther Mae jumping in to take care of him. They were intent on outbidding each other, but more focused on outbidding a young blonde who had apparently decided Emmett was the man to spend her money on.

As soon as Brady asked for more bids, Norma Sue shoved her hand in the air and glared at Esther Mae. "You might as well back off. Both of you."

Brady chuckled, acknowledged her bid and asked for more. "Who'll make it one-sixty?"

The young woman shot a perturbed look toward her competitors and then waved a bid.

Poor Emmett turned slightly green.

Stacy had shredded her paper napkin and was now

starting on Lynn's. "Why is she trying to get Emmett?" she whispered in alarm.

Lynn patted her arm. "It's all for a good cause. I wish you could bid but it'll be okay. Emmett only has eyes for you."

The younger woman was obviously looking for a date and knew a good thing when she saw it. The way she kept bidding, Lynn thought maybe she wasn't going to quit until she won him.

"Who'll give me one-seventy?"

"I will!" Esther Mae exclaimed, shaking her red head enthusiastically.

Emmett looked relieved.

The determined young woman was not happy and the minute Sheriff Brady rattled off the next amount she jumped to her feet. "I bid *two hundred!*"

"What?" Stacy gasped and ripped Lynn's napkin in half.

Chance and his family had been cheerfully rooting for the bidding, along with all the other people in the room. Lynn had been distracted by Chance and was finding it hard not to stare—the man had green eyes as vivid as cool creek water. She'd caught him watching her several times and each time butterflies had filled her chest. She found her gaze drawn back to him now, just as Brady called, "Two-twenty?" Chance tugged his ear!

She sat up straighter. Was that a bid? Had it not been for the fact that sharp-eyed Brady acknowledged it as such she might not have caught it. But he confirmed her suspicion by instantly accepting it and moving on to the next bid.

Esther Mae, Norma Sue and the determined blonde looked around to see who else had bid, but Chance gave no indication that it was him. If anyone else saw his inconspicuous bid they didn't give him away either.

He was good. As the next few minutes passed in heavy war Lynn was fascinated by him. When the bid hit two and fifty the blonde finally huffed and gave up. Norma Sue and Esther Mae searched the room to see who was bidding against them.

"Who is it?" Stacy whispered for the fourth time.

Brady was having a great time with the secret and Lynn couldn't help being happy about it, too. "It'll be okay," she assured Stacy.

Norma Sue's gaze landed on Chance as he nodded his head. Brady, a good auctioneer, had been careful not to make direct eye contact with Chance since he'd picked up that it was an anonymous bid. Norma Sue hiked a brow then grinned, crossed her arms and settled back in her seat without giving a bid. Not so quick to catch it, Esther Mae started to open her mouth but Norma Sue elbowed her, gave a hard shake of her head then whispered something to her.

"Oh! Ohh." Exclaimed the excitable redhead and with a chuckle she settled down, her mouth zipped up tighter than a vacuum seal.

"Going once, twice…"

Chance scratched his chin and Lynn saw his finger subtly pointing in Stacy's direction.

"Sold to anonymous third party and gifted to Stacy."

"What?" Stacy gasped the same moment that Emmett did.

The room ignited in a roar of good cheer.

"You won him, Stacy!" Lynn exclaimed, hugging her friend as Sheriff Brady's gavel slammed down on the podium.

"But I didn't bid."

"That's okay, someone did it for you as a donation. Now you can fix Emmett a good meal and he can help you with decorating the shelter. It's perfect."

That was the end of the auction and Lynn was relieved. She'd been tense as the cowboys were auctioned off. She'd heard what Chance's cousins had been saying and she was afraid one of them would do something crazy. But they had behaved.

"Well, that concludes our bachelor auction and we've raised a good amount of donations for the shelter tonight. Thank you all and I hope you ladies make these cowboys work hard for their suppers. As an added tag to the evening, earlier in the day we had a donation made to No Place Like Home by Wyatt, Seth and Cole Turner on behalf of their cousin. You all know Chance."

There was chair scraping as everyone shifted to stare at Chance. Lynn's stomach went south with an uneasy feeling. Chance sat up straight in his chair. As if reading her mind, his gaze shot to her then straight to Wyatt and the rest of his family. They were all grinning at him.

Lynn's cheeks began to burn even before anything else was said....

Sheriff Brady kept on talking. "The donation stipulation is a bonus for the evening. It seems that Chance has agreed to be auctioned off to Lynn Perry and her boys for an entire day of work at their new home. Let's give him a hand and everyone else who participated in the evening."

Lynn was floored. "I don't need help," she said, looking at Chance and the table of people responsible for this. Chance had a resigned expression that embarrassed her even more. It was obvious that he'd not volunteered to help her and her boys. And if the man didn't want to help she certainly didn't want his help. She hadn't asked for any, that was certain. If there was one thing she hated it was feeling needy. Oh, she had been there—very much in need—but she didn't like it. And right now she was in a position where she was helping herself, standing on her own two feet. That was a feeling she *liked*.

She did not need Chance Turner's help, nor that of his wealthy cousins!

It was one thing to help Stacy but this… *This is for the good of the shelter,* said a little voice in the back of her head.

She ignored it and marched straight over to the group. "Thank you for the thought. But I don't need the help." She tried to keep her rising irritation out of her voice. "I hope you'll give the donation to the shelter anyway."

Wyatt gave her a crooked grin, one that all the Turner men had in varying degrees. "Lynn, he's just coming out to hang some lights."

A heavy tug of embarrassment hit her. "I know that. It's just that I don't need any help." Her gaze slid to Chance, who still didn't look any happier about the situation.

Amanda looked worriedly at her. "We just thought with this being the Christmas season and you and the boys being in your own place that some help would be nice."

"And we wanted to make sure Chance didn't get

bored or become a hermit out there at the stagecoach house," Cole drawled. "If not for yourself, think of our poor cousin."

Chance shot Cole a long-suffering look. It was easy to tell he was used to being teased by his cousins. "Yeah, think of me," Chance said at last. "If you don't let them do this I'll never hear the end of it."

Not because he wanted to. "I don't think so." She refused to have a man working around her house who didn't want to be there. Especially when *she* didn't want him there in the first place. Despite her words everyone continued to watch her expectantly. Did they think this was all it took for her to be herded into their way of thinking? She had a mind of her own. "No thank you," she added more firmly for clarification. She had a right to make her own decision without feeling guilty about it! Before she acted like a total jerk, she turned and headed out the door with her back straight. She knew they were all probably thinking she was being rude but she couldn't help that. She and her boys could put up their own lights. They could.

She was within a few steps of escape when she heard her name.

"Lynn, wait." Norma Sue left Esther Mae talking to a relieved looking Emmett and a still baffled Stacy. "Did I hear you say you weren't going to accept Chance's help?"

People were milling around in groups and Lynn shuffled out of the way of a wave of folks talking excitedly among themselves. She glanced toward the door. "No, Norma Sue, I'm not."

"But you have to, honey. They paid that money and

it isn't going to hurt anything. And you really deserve some help, what with all you have going on, working, taking care of those boys, and the upcoming children's pageant."

The pageant wasn't going to be much trouble. The kids were practicing the songs on Sunday mornings and Adela and Esther Mae were doing the costumes, so all she had to do was oversee a dress rehearsal. No trouble at all. "Norma Sue, it's embarrassing," she confided. Norma Sue, Esther Mae and Adela had been wonderful to volunteer at the shelter. They'd kept children when needed and offered moral support and shoulders to cry on. In doing so Lynn and all the other women at the shelter had come to love them like family. They also knew that Lynn had issues—issues she didn't like to dwell on. Or talk about. They knew this. So why were they pressuring her?

"Don't get any ideas about me and…*him*. Don't you dare do it. I told you the other day not to." She whispered *him* long and hard, giving the notorious matchmaker a warning eye as uncomfortable thoughts of being alone with a man pressed in on her. She'd not let her thoughts dwell on old fears that hid deep inside her. She held her emotions in a tight coil.

This entire situation had matchmaking written all over it—just like she'd been afraid it would. Lynn hadn't realized until now that Wyatt Turner had hooked his brothers up with their wives before he himself fell in love and married Amanda. That being the case, it hit her instantly that he would want to see his cousin married off, too.

Surely not with me.

Surely yes, and she knew they were thinking it could work. Chance's stay in town would be his perfect opportunity. They had no idea how wrong they were. None... The room suddenly felt far too closed in... She swayed slightly and fought to stay calm as her past swept like a dark, clawing shadow choking her—like Drew had done so many times. She couldn't breathe. Couldn't think.

Esther Mae was heading their way like an excited bumblebee in her yellow-and-black velour jogging suit, followed by Adela. They were so happy with their good intentions. So totally misguided. Lynn pressed a hand to her stomach and demanded her body and her emotions not betray her but it was a losing battle. Suddenly, the room seemed to implode about her.

Breathe. Her pulse rate skyrocketed and her stomach plummeted. It was that weird, unkind feeling that had taken over in the midst of trying to escape the violence of her life. She'd thought that once she escaped her husband's fist she'd be okay. But that hadn't been the case. Her panic attacks had eased up over the last couple of years but this was a bad one.

She made it out the door in seconds, rushing off the plank sidewalk and around the side of the building, where she managed to fight off the need to throw up. Drew's twisted, violent face filled her mind's eye and she gagged. Her stomach rolled.

"Dear God, help me," she gasped, and stumbled toward her car. She had to get home. No one could see her like this. No one.

Almost before the words were out of her mouth she felt some semblance of control returning. Not completely, but a portion.

She headed down the street and felt relief as she reached her car.

Christmas was coming. This was the time to be happy and to count her blessings. She inhaled the cold, fresh air and willed her pulse to slow. It didn't. The last thing she needed to do was let this pull her down further. She thought of the good in her life. She had a great life going for her now.

Some women needed and wanted men in their lives. The only two men she *wanted* or *needed* in her life were her twins. They were the loves of her life and she was satisfied with that.

She did not need Chance Turner's family or anyone else, *including* Chance, interfering with the life she was envisioning for her and her boys.

And that included how she chose to decorate her house for Christmas!

"Lynn, wait."

No. She spun, startled by Chance's voice. "I need to go pick my boys up," she said, praying for strength in her words.

"Look, about what happened in there—"

Miraculously she calmed. "I won't be railroaded, Chance. And that's exactly how it felt in there. I'm the first to know the auction was for a great cause, but I would have bid on a man if I'd wanted one. And I didn't, don't and won't be forced, no matter how good the intention."

"And I'd have put myself in the running if I'd wanted a woman." He stopped a few steps from her. "Believe me, the last thing I want is to railroad you. I just came out here to say I'm sorry if we offended you. I know that is the last thing my family wanted to do. They thought they were doing you a favor—"

"They were trying to match us up."

He had the decency not to deny it. "You're right. I think that was apparent. But still, there was no offense intended. I can tell you're upset. Are you okay? Is there something I can do?"

She shook her head, tears suddenly threatening. "I—I'm not offended. Not really. Look, I have my own plans and I'm hoping everyone can understand that and honor my wishes."

"Yeah, sure they can. I'll relay that to my family." He stepped toward her, concern written in his expression. "You aren't okay."

"I'm fine." She pulled open her car door. "Don't worry about me. You have your own plan you came to town to work on, I'm sure." Why she added that she wasn't certain, but he got an odd look on his face. His jaw tightened and he glanced down the street for a long moment. Pain? Was that what she'd just seen?

When he looked back at her his eyes were troubled, confirming that she had just seen a flash of hurt. "I do have my reasons for being back here. Anyway, you be careful picking up your kids. The deer are getting hungry this time of year and probably thick along the roadways."

Her heart tightened for him as he headed down the street in the direction opposite from the community center. Apparently he'd had enough, too.

She got inside her car and sat in the silence, giving herself time to calm down before driving. This wasn't a new thing to her. She'd been upset far too many times in her life and knew driving while her world was spinning was risky.

She was still thinking about that troubled look in Chance's eyes when she finally headed to pick up the boys. Instead of worrying and dwelling on what had happened to her, she couldn't stop wondering what had brought Chance home.

She'd heard there had been a tragedy and a cowboy had been killed by the bull he'd been trying to ride. But that didn't explain why Chance had come home. He was a rodeo preacher—tragedy happened. And he was a man of faith. So what had put that pain in his expression… in his heart?

It was none of her business.

And she wanted it to remain that way. She did not want to get into Chance Turner's business and she didn't want him in hers.

Period.

With a capital *P*.

Chapter Six

Chance just couldn't let it go. Sitting in the truck at the end of Lynn's drive he stared at the house in the early morning sunlight.

It had a steep gable roof and a porch on the front with a matching roofline. It was one of those roofs that Christmas lights looked great on, but a man could break his neck hanging them on the high pitch. The thought of Lynn attaching those lights herself bothered him as he pressed the gas and drove down the gravel driveway. Not to mention the fact that he couldn't stop thinking about how upset she'd been last night. He'd noticed that even upset as she was she'd shown concern for him in the end.

Pulling to a halt in front of the house, he stepped from the truck and hesitated before striding to the porch. He'd come for a reason, not an excuse. *Not* because he hadn't been able to get her off his mind.

The boards creaked as he stepped on them and one—no, several—he noticed at closer inspection were in need of replacement. He knocked on the door and waited. When there was no answer after a couple of minutes he knocked again. Lynn's car was parked at the edge of the house in the metal carport so she had to be home.

It was likely that she'd peeked out the window, had seen him and decided not to open the door.

He hoped not though. On the other hand, he couldn't blame her if she did exactly that after everything that had transpired last night.

In the short time he'd been home the weather had gone from the forties to today's seventy degrees. It was a beautiful balmy December day in Texas—they were having a snowstorm up north and Texas was having a breezy summer day in the middle of the winter. It was one of those perks of living in the Lone Star State. He rapped his knuckles on the door one last time before heading back to his truck, more disappointed than he wanted to admit.

Laughter coming from behind the house called for a detour.

Careful to watch for running twins, he strode around the corner and spotted Lynn and both boys hard at work on what appeared to be the beginnings of a tree house. But the only indication it was a tree house was the fact that a tree was involved.

Their backs were to him, huddled together studying their handiwork. Lynn said something and the boys laughed.

A ball of unease settled in his gut. What was he doing?

The Catahoula was sprawled on its back off to the side enjoying the sunlight. He must have caught Chance's scent on the wind because he suddenly sprang to his feet, belted out a war cry and charged his way. Uh-uh. Not happening again. Chance braced himself, stared at the dog and commanded, "No."

Instantly Tiny dropped to his haunches and stared at him like a tiny puppy being scolded. His wide head cocked and his eyes pleaded an explanation but he sat still.

"Chance!" Gavin exclaimed first. Without waiting the boy raced toward him and grabbed him around the knees. "I told Momma you'd come help us."

"Hi, Gavin. What kind of help do you need?" The zealous greeting took Chance by surprise.

Jack was right on his brother's heels. "With the tree house," he exclaimed, latching on to his other leg. Despite the frown on Lynn's face there was no way Chance couldn't smile.

"So you're building that tree house. Sounds like fun!"

Without hesitation they each grabbed a hand, tugging him forward, chattering all the way. Tiny pounded about them in a circle barking excitedly. Chance had trouble following what they were saying: They were building a tree house, they found wood in the old barn, Gavin wanted to climb the ladder but his momma wouldn't let him, Jack couldn't hit a nail for nothin'! Chance laughed at that one.

It was amazing how much information poured out of them in the twenty feet between the house and the tree.

"Good morning," he said to Lynn. "It looks like you could use a little help." She might not want it but it was glaringly apparent that Lynn needed help with this project. Once again he felt bad for her—caught in a situation she didn't want and all because of him. She'd been nailing a board to a tree limb—he assumed this was going to be the floor of the tree house. He eyed it, not wanting to be critical, but he was really glad, for safety reasons, that the thing was only about five feet off the ground. Lynn was standing on a lightweight fiberglass ladder that she'd leaned against the limb. He didn't want to tell her that her structure wasn't going to be very safe.

"Hi," she said, climbing from the ladder. Her hair was in a ponytail and she wore a soft blue sweater that made her skin radiant. "I'm just starting."

He also didn't want to tell her that it didn't matter if she'd been working all day it wasn't going to get any better. "I was just passing by and thought I'd drop by. You know, see how you were this morning." He'd gone in for coffee at Sam's and been put through more of the same from Sam, App and Stanley. He couldn't explain in front of the twins that he needed to talk to her, so he left it at that. "This is going to be the floor, I'm thinking." He tried to sound light.

She didn't find that amusing. "We're learning."

"We got a mess." Jack crossed his little arms and studied the situation seriously. He looked like a miniature man contemplating his next move.

"Sure do," Gavin agreed. "Momma done nailed that board on there nine *hundred* times!"

Jack crunched his eyebrows looking up at Chance. "We're havin' a learn'n' experience, all right."

"Hey, it's not that bad." Lynn chuckled, and then sighed. "But close. Apparently I have no talent with a hammer and on top of that I have no clue what I'm doing. But we're getting there. We are definitely having a learning experience."

Chance felt for her. His own unease lessened a bit. "Can I talk to you for a minute?" He didn't want to talk about the money from the auction in front of the boys.

"Sure. Boys, why don't you go get a carton of juice. You deserve a break."

Both boys yelped excitedly and started toward the house only to halt.

"Are you gonna help us?" Gavin asked.

Chance felt a tug on his heartstrings. What did he say to that? He couldn't overstep their mother. "We'll see."

That got him two frowns. Lynn intervened. "Go on now and get your juice. You can add a cookie, too."

The offer was too sweet to pass up, bringing big grins as they raced each other to the back door. Tiny trailed them, flopping on the step to wait when they disappeared inside.

It was quiet the moment the door slammed shut behind them. Feeling suddenly ill at ease, Chance snagged his hat from his head and held it in both hands. "I came to tell you that my cousins gave the donation to the shelter with no strings attached. I didn't want you to feel bad or worry that your decision caused them not to get the money."

Her shoulders relaxed and her pretty eyes softened. "Thank you. I didn't want them to lose out on such a generous donation because I didn't accept the offer."

It was easy to see that she was a nice lady, just guarded. And hurt, giving her every right to protect herself. He couldn't help being curious about her. "I know we talked about this last night but I just want you to understand that my family meant well. They really did. They just overstepped their boundaries. The Turners are known for being overzealous at times. Or maybe the word is *overbearing*."

Lynn's shoulder lifted slightly. "Overzealous can be a good thing. I'm just into planning my own life these days. I hope people can understand that. If I hurt any feelings I'm sorry, but that's just the way it has to be."

Her back stiffened. She was closing the door between them again.

"You need to do what works best for you, Lynn." He glanced again at the poor tree house. "I could help if you'd like me to."

"No," she said too quickly. "We'll figure it out."

That was easy enough. And for the best, he guessed. "I'll head out then. I just wanted to tell you not to worry. You have a right to turn their offer down."

She nodded. He wondered why she was so wary. Of course it was easy to figure out that she came from an abusive situation, since she'd lived in the shelter. But how bad had it been? He'd seen the panic in her last night. Lynn looked strong. Nothing about her hinted that she would have allowed someone to lift a hand to her… but apparently she had. He knew that all too often there was a misconception that abused women were weak. That wasn't always true. He also knew there were ways to abuse someone other than physically.

No matter how much she pushed away his conversation, he couldn't get the idea out of his head. When she'd fled the building last night it had bothered him a great deal. He'd followed her but she hadn't been happy about it and had seemed glad to see him leave. He had a feeling she would be happy to see him leave now also.

He hadn't come home to Mule Hollow to hang around anyone. He'd come home for the solitude the ranch offered him. "Well, I guess I'll be drifting on out of here then." He tipped his hat and turned to go. It took all his considerable willpower not to offer once more to help...but considering that she wasn't even going to thank him for coming by, he decided keeping his mouth shut was the right option.

He was almost around the corner of the house when she called his name. Her voice was soft and there was a hesitancy to it that touched a chord inside him.

"Chance," she called again when he didn't immediately halt and look back. When he turned she hadn't moved.

"Thanks for stopping by. And..." She raked a hand over her hair. In the morning sunlight it gleamed like the blue-black coat on a raven. "...And thanks for understanding."

He nodded, then got out of there. She had not asked for his help and hadn't looked as if she had any plans to do so. The lady had simply said thank you.

It should have been the easy out he was hoping for. He'd taken the easy out with Randy and the bull rider had come up dead. This wasn't the same and he knew it, but that didn't stop him from thinking about Lynn all the way back to the ranch. One thing was certain. He'd come here for peace and solitude. He'd come here to get away from God and everyone else.

Except God wasn't having any of it.

But then Chance already knew that it didn't matter

whether a person was mad at God, or stumbling in the dark. God was always there waiting. Calling His own back to Him.

It was Chance who wasn't ready to let go. He felt as if he'd helped kill a man—some would say he was crazy for thinking such a thing. But that was how he felt. Randy might have gotten mixed up with the wrong crowd and avoided Chance in the last few weeks before his death, but Chance knew in his heart that despite the bad feeling he'd had about Randy, he'd not heeded God's nudge to seek Randy out. He had not gone the extra mile to help the young cowboy, who was clearly in a danger zone. It wasn't something Chance could forget or forgive. And no matter who said he wasn't responsible, in his heart of hearts he felt like God was holding him accountable. He felt like he'd failed Randy and God at the same time.

Emotionally and mentally Chance was not in a place to entertain thoughts of the single mother of two. But no matter what he did, Lynn continued to enter his head.

The heavy scent of rich, dark chocolate filled the candy shop. Lynn added sugar to the commercial-size pot and stirred. "No, I didn't accept the offer. Come on, don't you two give me a hard time."

Stacy bit her lip as Lynn and Nive Abbot squared off across the counter. Lynn didn't miss the way Stacy tensed at the very idea of her friends having words. Though she was wrong—Nive and Lynn weren't having words. They were simply having an excitable conversation.

"I'm not pushing in that way," Nive said, holding her plastic-gloved hands up in surrender. "I understand you aren't looking for a man but some help around the house from a man of God…that sounds like a plan to me. You know, I never thought about marrying a preacher but, hey, have you looked at that guy? Whoa! He has dreamy green eyes."

Lynn prayed for patience. "I'm not interested in his help, but I'm not dead. Who wouldn't notice his eyes?"

"They are nice," Stacy interjected, slicing the fudge in front of her.

Stacy already had cold feet about getting married. That was the only way Lynn could describe her reluctance to hire a preacher to come marry them. Yes, she was crazy in love with Emmett in her gentle, timid way, but she had spoken of recurring doubts that plagued her. The fact that Lynn was so against letting a man into her life wasn't helping matters. Lynn had noticed a change the instant she'd walked into the candy store that morning. She felt horrible that her decision was having a detrimental effect on the future of Stacy and Emmett. She hoped Nive would get the hint and clam up.

"I saw him watching you," Stacy added, pausing in her steady slicing. She smiled timidly. "A lot."

Her softly spoken words startled Lynn. "Watching me?" she asked. She'd noticed it herself but thought it was just because she couldn't seem to keep her eyes off him.

Stacy nodded her paper-cap-covered head and began slicing again. "He kept glancing your way over and over again. I think he looks sad."

"Me, too," Nive said. "I saw it in his yummy eyes. When he wasn't looking totally perplexed by his cousins teasing him. I heard something bad happened at one of the rodeos he was at. I think a bull rider was killed during his ride."

Lynn concentrated on stirring the chocolate mixture. Burning the bonbons wouldn't be good but her thoughts were not on her job. "I heard something similar—it was terrible. I meant to ask Norma Sue but too much other stuff was going on. I don't understand why cowboys want to get on the back of one of those killers. And my boys talk about becoming bull riders. I hate it." She cringed at the thought of her babies growing up and climbing on one of those huge monsters.

"It's a wonder more of them aren't killed," Stacy said.

"I know they know the risk they're taking but I just can't stand it. It would have to be hard on someone like Chance who was working with them." A mental picture of Chance witnessing to the riders week after week popped into her mind. It was easy to see that he would be a caring and compassionate preacher. And yet he had said he wasn't preaching right now. Whatever had happened had affected him deeply. She'd glimpsed sadness when he'd followed her to her car. It was there, along with the kindness she'd seen in the depths of his lush green eyes.

Okay, so maybe thinking of his eyes as lush wasn't the best way to put the man out of her head. But they were. The color didn't make her think of hard green stones but tall grass swaying gently in the breeze. As a little girl she'd always begged her mother to pull over when she saw a field of high grass tossed in the wind. It had looked like the perfect, safe place to run to. A perfect

place to find peace. Funny how she hadn't thought of
that in a very long time.

*The Lord makes me lie down in green pastures, He
leads me beside quiet waters, He restores my soul.* The
passage from Psalms echoed through her like a gentle
whisper that lifted her spirit. God had brought her a
long way from that childhood innocence. He'd carried
her through darkness and into the light. She wondered
if Chance was struggling in the darkness right now?

Men of God struggled. It was foolish to think they
never had pain...but that was none of her concern. He
had family and friends here who she was quite certain
were helping him with any problem he might be having.
He didn't need her worrying over it.

"I wonder if Chance would marry me and Emmett?"
Stacy asked.

It was the same thought that Lynn had had when she'd
first met Chance outside the church.

"That would be a great idea," Nive said excitedly,
pausing in the midst of wrapping the freshly sliced fudge
in colorful cellophane. It would be decorated with ribbon
in preparation for the gift shops they supplied all across
several counties.

Lynn removed the pot from the heat but kept stirring.
"Actually, I asked him about that and he said he wasn't
preaching right now."

Stacy turned hopeful blue eyes to her and it was easy
to see her disappointment. She had hoped to wait until
a preacher took over the pulpit who would mean something in their lives through the years. She didn't want
to have a stranger marry her. When she wasn't having
moments of cold feet, this marriage meant the world to

Stacy. "This is my new beginning. My fresh and beautiful union that I desperately want God to be a part of..." Her voice trembled and she went back to work. "I just don't understand. I want God involved in my wedding and that starts with the pastor who recites our vows. Why do I keep coming up against closed doors?"

Lynn couldn't stand the frustration in Stacy's voice. She closed her eyes and asked God to help her make this happen for Stacy. Opening her eyes she met Stacy's gaze and, despite her need to back away, Lynn knew what she had to do.

She was going to ask Chance Turner once more.

Chapter Seven

The sun had just peeked over the distant treetops when Chance saddled Ink and rode out of the barn. They'd ridden for a good hour, checking fence line, looking at the cattle and simply riding. Ink's ears had been back and he'd been jumpy at first, but now the black gelding had relaxed. Chance had, too, feeling the tension ease from him as he rode across the plains on the Turner ranch. Hauling from one rodeo to the next could wear on horse and man. Being at peace and roaming the wide-open space was good for both of them.

He'd awakened bound in his sheets and sweating bullets with Randy on his mind again. He couldn't stop thinking about that last ride. He had witnessed to Randy, told him that no one knows what the future holds, and he'd asked Randy once more to commit his life to the Lord. But it had been a no-go. Instead, Randy had wrapped his gloved hand with the bull rope, gripped it tightly and then grinned. "Not today," he'd said. "This is gonna be a good ride."

Chance saw his unfocused eyes in that instant and

got the uneasy feeling that tragedy was in the making. But the gate opened and it was too late.

How many times he'd replayed in his mind yanking Randy out of that box and stopping that ride.

Bull riders at the top of their game were athletes. They trained hard and respected their bodies and clear minds. You didn't ride against the toughest bulls—bulls with bigger reputations than the cowboys in many ways— without being prepared. Bull riders died all the time. It was a risk they accepted and they knew not being sharp upped their risk of death. But injuries caused problems. Ever since his shoulder injury two months earlier, Randy had come around more, asking questions. Chance had sensed a need in Randy to change his life. And yet he hadn't done it. Instead he'd continued hanging with a rough crowd to play with a lifestyle that Chance knew from his personal experience led only to dead ends and heartache. Why hadn't he done more for Randy? Why?

Chance was heading home, as unsatisfied as when he'd headed out, when he saw a car approaching the stagecoach house. He recognized Lynn Perry's aging auto as it drew closer. The vehicle had seen better days, but he figured Lynn was probably doing her best raising two boys on her own and putting a roof over their heads. There was much about Lynn to admire. He'd thought about that yesterday when he'd stopped to stare at the moon before calling it a night. She seemed very level-headed and in forward motion. He liked that about her. She was cautious about giving the wrong impression to men. And with reason. She'd been hurt before and now he'd seen it in her eyes—she didn't plan on being hurt again. He also figured she was looking out for her kids. A person didn't take all the risks involved in fleeing an abusive husband only to jump right back into a relationship. Not when she'd been trying to protect her kids in the first place.

So why was she here? He urged his horse forward across the space separating them. By the time he made it into the yard she'd gotten out of her car. She shielded her eyes from the glare of morning sun and watched him ride in.

She was beautiful standing there, and his heart lifted looking at her, beating out a bongo rhythm despite everything he knew about her and everything he'd come here to escape.

She gave him a terse smile as he approached. Clearly she was disturbed about being here.

"Hi." He dismounted as he spoke. As soon as his boots hit the ground he tipped his hat and couldn't help smiling at her. He suddenly felt the weight on his shoulders ease up. "I'm a little surprised to see you way out here. But I have to say I'm glad to see you."

"I'm surprised to be here, too," she said, unsmiling.

"But obviously not happy about it." He couldn't help teasing her.

She tugged the collar of her jacket closer around her chin and continued to look ill at ease. He waited for her to continue. The edge of her dark hair lifted from her cheek in the chilly breeze and she sucked in a breath. Serious eyes watched him.

"Is something wrong?" he asked.

"No. I'm sorry. I'm just…not sure how to do this."

His lips lifted and he gave her his best smile. She

wasn't the easily flustered type and yet she was now. The idea that she was flustered just being around him set his heart to pounding all over again. *In your dreams, Turner.* "I promise not to bite. Say what's on your mind."

She nodded and took a breath. "Gavin smashed his finger this morning when I was getting ready for work."

"Is he all right?"

"Yes, but…" She rubbed her temple and looked away momentarily. "But I feel horrible."

"Little boys like working on tree houses. There are hard lessons sometimes, but you have two very creative little boys who clearly want to learn. He'll be all right, that one."

He had no doubt about it. Her boys were determined little tykes. He'd thought his words would reassure her but they didn't. She shifted from one foot to the other and looked more distressed.

"He wasn't working on the tree house. He and Jack had moved that old ladder we found in the barn from the tree to the house. I don't know how they managed to get it standing against the house but they did."

This was going south quickly. "He didn't?"

"Gavin climbed the thing to the eaves and was trying to hang Christmas lights." Distress sounded loud and clear in her voice. "It's a wonder he hadn't fallen and hurt himself. He's only four—well, more five than four, but still. He could have been hurt because I'm so stubborn and want to do everything my way."

Chance stepped closer to her and had the urge to tug her into his arms and comfort her. Instead he smiled, hoping to ease her anxiety, though he was more concerned about the situation than she could know. "God took care of him, it seems. So don't beat yourself up over it."

"Easier said than done." Her lip curved slightly. "I seem to have made a mess of things. They wanted lights on our house for our first Christmas, but I got side-tracked trying to help them build a tree house—which is a disaster. By the time I figured out that I stink at carpentry it was too late to hang the lights. I haven't had time since to get them up. This is what happens when they decide they need to do things themselves."

She was upset. No two ways about it. She was a mother alone with a lot riding on her shoulders. Not only raising her two boys and providing for them but also overcoming whatever had sent her to the women's shelter. Chance wondered again what kind of heartache she'd gone through. And what kind of effects lingered from the past. "Come on, let's go sit down and let me get you a glass of tea." When she didn't move he took her arm. "Come on."

She took a deep breath and let him lead her to the porch. He opened the door and led her inside. The stage-coach house had a long, wide hall from front to back, its walls lined with old photos, some dating all the way back to the eighteen hundreds. He led the way into the living room, which was connected to the kitchen and separated by a large wooden table that had been here, as far as they knew, from the beginning. He liked the place. Its rustic stone fireplace and scuffed wooden floors were right up his alley. Their link to the past made it more special. "What can I do?" he asked as he pulled a chair out for her, then got a glass and filled it with ice from the automatic ice dispenser—there were a few modern conveniences that he enjoyed.

Relief and a mixture of embarrassment, if he was reading her expression correctly, washed over her. "I was wondering if that offer of your services was still open."

He pulled a pitcher of tea from the icebox as excitement hummed through him at the idea. He filled the glass and set it in front of her. "Yes, ma'am, it is." He sat down across from her. "And even if it had time limitations I'd be honored to help out you and your boys."

It was the truth. He and God might be having a difference of opinion right now, but that didn't matter when it came to down-home decency. This was the right thing to do. It was easy to see she was still struggling. Was it the idea that she needed help at all that was bothering her?

"Thank you so much," she said, taking a sip of her tea. "I'm sorry I lost it. I'm not usually so upset, but all the way out here I kept thinking about what a close call Gavin and Jack had. Gavin dropped his hammer and it almost hit Jack. My stomach keeps getting sick thinking about it."

He automatically covered her hand with his. "I'm sorry you had to go through that alone." Her hand was soft and he was tempted to keep holding it but drew his back. He sure liked the touch of her though.

"The boys will be ecstatic," she said, tucking her hands into her lap. "And despite all my efforts, your family, my friends and the matchmakers seem to be brewing up ideas about us with every passing moment. It worries me."

He hadn't mixed up any signals from Lynn, but his manly pride was getting a bit defensive that she'd easily dismissed the idea of being set up with the likes of him.

"As far as I'm concerned they can brew all they want. If I'm not interested in becoming involved in a relationship, I won't get involved. No matter who's doing the pushing." Was that a flicker of feminine prickle he saw in her eyes at the notion that he'd so blatantly refused involvement? If so she hid it well, because the next instant her lip crooked upward.

"Good. We're on the same page. What day will be best for you to come out?"

"I guess since you've got four-year-olds trying to scale your roof I'd better start as soon as possible. How's today?"

"Today—I'm sure you had something planned for today, penning cows or working them or something. Honestly, I'm not much of a cattle woman so I'm not really sure what all you do to them, but whatever you had planned I hate to take you away from it."

She was cute. He hadn't figured the slightly uptight lady for being cute, but she was. Sure, she was pretty, but a woman could be pretty and have no cuteness about her. "I had the big plans of just hanging out here by myself. I can do that tomorrow if you'll let me hang lights today." It hit him then that he was glad for the excuse not to be alone with his thoughts anymore today.

She smiled and he felt good… He hadn't felt good since before the day Randy leaned forward too far over B-par's back, and the hulking bull's powerful head had slammed into Randy's face full force. The move had dazed him and when he hit the ground B-par continued—

"If you're sure," he said, pushing the thoughts away and focusing on her.

"I'm sure." Something about the entire situation drew him. The last thing he'd expected to do when he came home was spend time with anyone, especially a pretty woman and two little boys. But it looked as if that was exactly what he was about to do. And as downhearted as he was feeling, the idea brightened his day more than he could say.

More than he deserved.

"I gots a smushed thumb under here." Gavin lifted his hand and showed off the bandaged thumb.

"I guess you learned about climbing all the way up there." Chance nodded toward the eave of the house where he was about to begin work hanging the boys' Christmas lights. Lynn had worked until two and then picked the kids up from the shelter. She'd explained that the women took turns at the shelter watching the children so that everyone could work in the candy store.

He could have come earlier but he'd felt it important to let the boys be a part of putting the lights on their home for the first time. When he'd chosen to do that, Lynn had looked pleased. Though she hadn't voiced the words, he got the feeling he'd earned points by wanting to include them. He wasn't looking for points or getting on her good side—that hadn't been his objective. He'd simply known the boys would have fun and he would enjoy their help. He also wanted to talk to them about the dangers of climbing a ladder.

"I wasn't scared. Jack told me he didn't wanna do it."

Jack shook his head back and forth in methodical rhythm, as if he were watching a tennis match. "My stomach hurts when I get too high. I told Gavin not to do it. But I held the ladder for him, like I seen Miss Dottie do for Sheriff Brady when he was workin' on the barn roof."

"Only when I dropped the hammer it done almost hit Jack on the head!"

Chance got a vivid picture of the little dude holding the ten-foot ladder and dodging the hammer.

"Momma said it was a *miracle* I didn't fall when I smashed my thumb."

"And another miracle the hammer didn't hit me in the head."

Chance's heart clutched at the thought…the same way he felt looking back on Randy's last ride. He hadn't done anything about Randy's situation but he could do something here.

The idea coursed through him like a wildfire. He tamped it down. These were just little boys wanting to be handy around the house. Randy had been hyped up on drugs, strapped to the back of one of the most ferocious bulls on the circuit. It had been a deadly combination…a train wreck in the making and he hadn't seen it coming. But maybe there was some redemption here helping Gavin and Jack.

Maybe he could make a small difference in these boys' lives by at least getting up the Christmas lights they'd been talking about since the day they'd first run him over.

The memory made him smile. "You boys are all right. You know that?"

They beamed at the praise just as Lynn came out the front door. She'd gone inside to change out of her slacks into jeans and an oversize, cream-colored sweater that hung below her hips. She'd pulled her hair into a ponytail once more and Chance missed the way it hung around her face. She also had changed from boots to canvas shoes that had seen better days. The outfit looked as if she had loved and worn it for years.

He sure missed her hair hanging down though, no matter how much he tried not to think about it.

"Did you come to help, too, Momma?" Jack asked.

"Sure did." She hugged him and gave him a kiss on the head, making him giggle. "Is that okay with you fellas?"

Gavin crunched his brows together skeptically. "Long as you don't use the hammer. You're worse with it than me."

"Hey!" Lynn laughed cheerily. "That's not a nice thing to say about your ol' momma." She engulfed him in a swooping hug and growled against his neck. He squealed and wiggled attempting to escape.

Jack hopped from foot to foot excitedly. "Get him, Momma! Get him."

Chance had climbed the first two rungs of the ladder but paused to watch them. They were good together. The three of them. Lynn had done a great job. She should be very proud of herself. Laughing and breathless from romping with Gavin she let him go and smiled at Chance. Her cheeks were soft pink and she had a happy glow about her as she held his gaze. His stomach tilted looking down at her and he felt peaceful.

"I wish I had some of those plastic gadgets you hang lights with. It would make things a lot easier, I think."

He held up the staple gun. "We'll do it the old-fashioned way."

"You ain't usin' a hammer?"

"Nope, Gavin, I'm afraid I'd hit my thumb if I tried to hang lights with a hammer."

"You don't want ta do that. It hurts."

"Yeah, I reckon it did." He climbed the ladder carrying a strand of lights and all three jumped to hang on to the ladder.

"We won't let you fall, Mr. Chance," Jack yelled at the top of his lungs.

"Thanks. I'm in good hands. I can see that."

"There are none better than my boys," Lynn called, her voice bright with affection.

Chance looked down to find her smiling up at him as she said the words. She looked so pretty and so happy at that moment that he almost missed a rung on the ladder.

Chapter Eight

"So, what do you think?" Chance asked as he hopped to the ground. He'd hung several strands of lights, and the old house was looking great.

He was standing close to Lynn and she could feel the warmth from his body through the down vest that he wore. She'd helped him for the last hour and he'd been great with her boys. And, okay, the man smelled wonderful.

"Momma, don't ya got yor ears on? What do you think?" Jack asked, tugging on her arm. It was what she always asked him and Gavin when they weren't listening to her.

Boy, where had she been? How embarrassing was that? "Ear one and ear two are both on and ready to do their jobs," she said lightly, careful not to look at Chance.

She hoped Chance hadn't noticed her embarrassing lapse. She stole a glance at him. He caught her and the wink he gave her said he'd noticed plenty.

"You were taking a nap," he drawled, a teasing smile

tugging at his lips as he grabbed the ladder and moved it down three feet.

A flutter erupted inside her chest at his words and she watched him. He moved with an athletic grace she'd been admiring all morning.

Leaning the ladder against the house, he placed a hand on his hip and grinned. "Seriously, I think a mother of active twin boys deserves to grab a power nap any time she can get it."

"Thanks, they are few and far between." Her mouth felt like she'd stuffed marshmallows in it when he gave her a crooked grin.

"Hey, remember I'm the hired help, so if you need to go grab a little shut-eye I'd be more than glad to watch these two cowpokes of yours."

"Oh, that is so tempting." True, she wasn't looking for a romance. Or a date even. But there was nothing keeping her from liking the guy. And the more she knew of him, the more she liked him.

"I'm serious," he said, looking at the boys, who were stretching out the strands of lights like he'd shown them, checking for burned-out bulbs. Jack plugged one end into an extension cord. "We've got this."

The thing was that, as a single working mom of two active boys, she literally dreamt of sleeping… "No. I'm good. I want to do this with the boys." *And you.* So she was human. She was a woman drawn to a man. But that was all. Nothing more.

He grinned and it was like a bolt of sunshine. "Sounds great to me."

What was a great guy like Chance Turner doing still single? The man had never been married and he was about twenty-eight, if she had her figures straight. He was a year older than Cole and they'd had a small gathering for Cole's birthday three weeks ago. Not that being twenty-eight and never married was a bad thing. She assumed his lack of a wife had a lot to do with being on the road so much.

Not that it mattered to her one way or the other. He was simply a nice guy who was kind to her kids.

And you're having a great time with him.

"Hey, Chance, got one," Gavin yelled, waving at him to come to the end of the strand.

"It's blown, all right," Jack added.

"Duty calls." He tipped his hat, eyes twinkling. "Want me to show you how to change a bulb, too?"

"Sure, sounds great," she laughed, her heart feeling as light as the breeze blowing in across the yard.

She watched him show the boys how to replace a bulb with one of the extras in a little plastic bag that was still attached to the strand.

Her boys huddled with him, their little brown and blond heads bent next to his black one. When the light popped on like the rest of them they whooped and gave each other high fives. Guys.

"There ain't nothin' to that," Gavin gushed.

Chance grinned at him. "You're right. It's easy once you know how to do it."

"What if there's not any extras with the lights?" Jack asked, looking at the strand that lay next to them.

"You can get a little pack of them for less than a dollar, I think."

"Did you hear that, Momma? I got a dollar. I can help."

"I got a dollar, too, Jack," Gavin added, not wanting to be outdone.

"And that is one reason I love you two so much, because you are my little helpful men."

They beamed at the praise and Chance winked at her once more. There was nothing meant by the wink other than agreement with what she'd said, but that didn't stop her insides from feeling suddenly as if she'd been turned upside down. She stepped back, having somehow moved to stand a bit too close to him.

"I guess I'd better get dinner started. You're upholding your part of the deal so I'd better get mine together. Do you like King Ranch chicken?"

"Does a horse like sweet feed? It's my favorite."

A warm bloom of pleasure spread through her at the way he was smiling at her. Self-conscious, she glanced at her boys, who looked in shock at each other, then up at him.

"It's our favorite, too!" Gavin exclaimed for both of them, and Jack nodded, his big blue eyes locked on Chance in admiration.

Shaken by the attachment that her boys seemed to have formed so quickly, she had to force her voice to sound normal. "Then while you boys are finishing up I'll go start on that." She should have already started it, but she'd been unable to walk away from hanging the lights.

It was nice seeing her boys with a good man. The neighbors had helped with several projects at the shelter. Men like Dan Dawson, who'd lived in a shelter growing up, came by to play football and hang out. And others like Mule Hollow deputy Zane Cantrell spent time with the boys, especially after he'd married Rose, who'd lived in the shelter with them. And there were all the others like Clint Matlock, Pace Gentry and Cort Wells who helped the boys with their riding skills. The list went on and on. Mule Hollow was full of great cowboys and everyone she'd thought about was now happily married to friends of hers. The single guys came around too, and it never failed to bless her soul to see men willing to mentor kids who weren't lucky enough to have a man in their life. It was special.

So why, she asked herself with one last glance before heading inside, did it seem her boys had latched on to Chance Turner like they'd never before latched on to anyone?

Chance was having a hard time concentrating. He'd helped with the lights and had a blast with the boys. They were quick learners and interested in everything. While Lynn had cooked supper they'd taken him to the backyard tree house. Chance didn't want to think or say anything derogatory but there was no denying that they needed an intervention.

He'd crossed his arms and studied the poor thing. The boys flanked him and he bit back a laugh when he realized they were copying his own stance.

How easy it was to influence those around you. He'd made a lot of mistakes in his rebellious wild days, during the beginning of his riding career. It had taken one fateful night—a bar brawl had gone bad and a drunk had pulled a knife on him and a riding buddy. Thankfully, his buddy had lived after being stabbed and in the emergency room Chance had come to know the Lord.

That E.R. doctor had intervened in more than a physical crisis. He'd also stepped in and brought Chance to his knees before the Lord. Ever since then, Chance had tried his best to be the man that God had intended for him to be. He'd wanted to be like Doc Stone…a man who stood in the gap and boldly told others about God.

He'd made plenty of mistakes along the way. But that hadn't stopped him from trying, striving to be a man of integrity, one the rough-and-tumble riders could see living his witness, day in and day out.

Looking at the boys standing beside him gave him a reprieve from the feeling of failure that had weighed on his shoulders since Randy's death. He knew it was temporary and undeserved, but he wasn't able to walk away from these two without offering to help them on the tree house, too. Even if the solitude he craved called to him back at the stagecoach house.

"It's a sad situation, ain't it," Gavin said, solemnly.

"Hopeless," Jack sighed heavily.

Even Tiny looked depressed about the scary way the boards tilted between the tree limbs.

"It's not hopeless." All three—dog included—looked at him with hope. There was no way he couldn't help. *No way.* "All it's going to take is a little know-how. Your momma has never built one of these before, but I'd give her an A for effort anyway."

"Yeah, she tried." Gavin let out a long sigh.

"You did um, ain't ya," Jack said, sounding more and more like Applegate.

"Yes, I have, Jack. But my first one was a disaster, too."

"Worse than ours?"

Chance laughed. "Yes, Jack. Worse than yours. But, see, my uncle had to come help me and my cousin Cole rebuild it. We couldn't do it on our own."

"Your uncle helped you. Not your dad?" Gavin was studying him, probing. The look in his eyes pulled at Chance's heartstrings.

"No, not my dad. It was my uncle." His dad had spent a good deal of time away from him.

"We don't got a dad to help us either," Gavin continued and Jack nodded.

Chance swallowed the lump that formed in his throat. He'd been too young at the time to realize that it wasn't normal for a kid to spend so much time away from his dad. And his mom. He'd had his cousins and his uncle and aunt to fill in the holes. He'd been lucky. It wasn't until he was a little older that he understood. "You don't have a dad, but God gave you a mom who loves you and tries very hard. That's the best thing ever."

"Yup," Jack sighed. "That's good, ain't it, Gavin?"

"Yup."

As if that was all that needed to be said on the subject, they went back to studying the dilapidated tree house.

"So what do ya say? Do you want me to help you?" He knew the minute the words were out of his mouth and the boys turned jubilant smiles up at him that he was in trouble.

Chapter Nine

"Well, that was some day and a great meal," Chance said. He and Lynn were standing on the front porch and he was getting ready to head home. They'd gotten most of the Christmas lights up and had a meal better than anything he'd eaten in a long time. Lynn Perry could cook.

"Thanks. I can make a few dishes pretty decently. But I'm pretty iffy on the rest."

He laughed and looked down at her. He was getting partial to looking into her deep blue eyes. He kept finding himself trying to figure out what she was thinking and feeling. When she looked at her boys it was clear as blue skies what she was thinking. But it was the rest of the time that had him hooked.

"I know you're being humble now. There is no way you can cook a dish that mouthwatering and not be able to cook anything else you wanted. That was awesome. Really, Lynn."

In the porch light, she looked pleased. His gaze dropped to her lips, full and expressive, their corners tight with uncertainty. Her lips. Chance pulled back, tugged his jacket closed and stuffed his hands into his pockets—for safety. He'd been thinking about pulling her into a hug and kissing her. That's what you did at the end of a date—but that was just it, this was not a date.

He wasn't here for a date.

But that was exactly what it had felt like sitting around her kitchen table with her two sons enjoying her excellent King Ranch chicken.

"Well, I guess as a mom, I'm just happy the boys like my cooking." She had pulled on a coat when she'd walked him outside. Now she tugged it close and took a deep breath.

He did the same as silence stretched between them. It was time to go but he was reluctant. He felt more at peace right now than he had in what seemed like ages. Part of that had come from her, and part from the boys. They'd touched a chord in him that he hadn't even known was there. He'd bent down and given them a hug before they'd gone to take their bath. And they'd asked him once more about the tree house, their excitement overflowing.

"So you're fine with me working on the tree house?"

"I don't want to impose. But the boys are so excited."

"You can say that again." He chuckled. "I don't have anything pressing right now. And I enjoyed today…and don't think I'm not getting something from it. It was good for me."

It had been very good for him.

In the porch light her blue eyes darkened. "Are you all right? I heard you came home because of something to do with that bull rider who was killed."

He shifted his weight from one boot to the other and hefted a shoulder. "Randy was his name."

"You were close?"

Chance rubbed the edge of a curling porch board with his boot and fought a tightness in his chest. "I'd been witnessing to him. I'd known him for a while though he was only twenty-five. I felt responsible for him."

"It must have been really hard on you."

"Yeah." He inhaled the chilling air, feeling cold to the bone. "Harder on Randy. He just needed a little more time."

She startled him by placing a hand on his arm. He could feel the warmth of it through his jacket. The simple act warmed his heart more than any words could have.

"You could only do what you could do. You can't make choices for other people."

His mood shifted suddenly and he gave a harsh laugh. "Boy, don't I know it."

She squeezed his arm and then tucked her hand back into her jacket. He felt colder instantly.

"I know what you're feeling about that," she said. "If it had been up to me I'd have made several decisions for others in my life. But it wasn't possible. For my children, yes, and I made the most important one for them when I took them to the shelter in L.A. I know that I only have them for a short season in life and then they'll be on their own. I'll be praying that I did everything and gave them everything I could to help them make the right choices. That's all you could do for your friend. For Randy."

He hadn't told anyone else how he felt about the drugs.

Other than Wyatt. "I could have done more, intervened about the prescription drugs and the bad decisions he was making."

"Maybe, but maybe not."

He nodded. "Look, it's cold. You better get back inside. Thanks for the evening. And the company." He had to move. The guilt was on him once more like a heavy shroud.

"Chance, wait."

His heart thumped against his ribs when he turned to find her right beside him. "Please do come build the tree house," she said and then she took his breath completely away when she hugged him. As easily as the breeze, she slipped her arms around his waist and hugged him tightly. Her face rested against his heart as she held on to him. She was warm and soft and smelled so sweet. And she was holding him.

By the time he tugged his hands from his coat pockets she was stepping back.

"Come tomorrow if you can. I get off at two again," she said, smiling. She slipped inside the house.

Tiny, who'd been flopped across the bottom step, lumbered over to whine at the door.

Chance didn't move at all. Not for a full minute.

He just stood there staring at the door.

"You hugged him!"

"Well, Nive, you had to have been there. He just needed it."

"Hey, I didn't ask why. I'm all for it. When he gets there this afternoon, you going to hug him again?"

"No. I just did it on the spur of the moment. He

looked so sad. He feels responsible for Randy's death. Even though you and I both know we can't be responsible for someone else's actions." They'd both learned that after years of letting abusive husbands make them think it was their fault they were getting beaten. It just didn't work that way. For anyone.

"So the kids really like him." Nive leaned over the glass counter and put her chin in her palm. Her amber-colored hair was pulled into a messy topknot and loose tendrils fell around her heart-shaped face.

"It's scary how they've attached to him."

"It's cool. Wonderful."

Lynn frowned. "Nive—"

"Don't look at me that way. Do you seriously not think you're going to remarry?"

Lynn laid her pencil down, finished with the list she was making. "In my heart of hearts I just can't see it happening. I mean, well, you know how it is. Those two precious boys are my responsibility. What if I made a mistake? What if I could trust a man again and he… and it turned out bad. I don't want to think about it."

"Are you sure you aren't just using them as an excuse?"

"Maybe." She was honest about it. "Because I sure can't read my mixed-up heart. The one thing I'm positive about in life are my boys." She loved them and they loved her and they were her life. And God loved them. She was certain about that also. So two things. Three— God had brought them here. It was good. So there were plenty of things she was sure of, but she wasn't sure that she could ever truly open up to a man and be a wife, emotionally, physically, mentally. She had baggage even she didn't like looking at.

If she did find a good man he would deserve more than she could give him.

"Well, I think it's great you're going to let him help you with that tree house. Gavin and Jack told me it was horrible."

"The little toots!"

Nive made a face. "Seriously, Lynn. You weren't going to let them walk around on those boards after you nailed them in? Jack said you nailed one in and it fell right off the tree and stuck in the ground. Those were his very words."

"All the more reason to be glad I decided to let Chance help."

"How's the Christmas shopping going? Did you get a tree yet?"

"Nive, I just got the lights up. Hopefully we'll get a tree this weekend, because next weekend is pageant practice. I've got to go. Wish me luck. I'm going to talk to Chance this afternoon about Stacy's wedding if the time seems right. I really think he'll do it. He's just hurting right now. But I feel like if I just explain everything he'll do it."

Nive didn't move from her position but lifted a hand and waved. "I'll say a prayer. I want that girl married so bad it's not funny. If ever there was a need for a happy ending it's for Stacy... I'd even give up dreaming about my own if Stacy-girl could have hers."

"That's really sweet of you, Nive. But don't worry. I feel like God has this under control."

"Hey, He might have more than you think under

control where you and this cowboy preacher are concerned."

Lynn was opening the door when Lacy practically waddled in. Her blond, erratically wavy hair framed her adorable face and she looked a little puffy under the eyes.

"How are you?" Lynn asked, pulling the door closed to keep the cold out.

"Priscilla is kicking like an Olympic soccer player. She needs a container of peanut brittle. Now!"

Nive was already moving. "Tell her to hold her horses. I'm getting it."

"You have eaten your weight in peanut brittle," Lynn said.

"Yep, yep, yep, and I've enjoyed every ounce of it! I'm holding up my bargain and I'm off to kick my feet up at home, munch on peanut brittle and let Priscilla watch a little *Love Me Tender*. That Elvis movie's got some soothing music in it, so maybe the little whirlwind will settle down and stop kicking."

"You and Elvis." Lynn laughed. She had her Elvis-pink Caddy and loved his music. "Do you think if you stopped feeding her so much sugar it might help?"

"Hey, I'm monitoring my sugar intake. I'm not eating it in anything but candy."

"*Lacy*," Lynn gasped. "You're so bad."

"Hey, I'm a pregnant woman." She took the bag Nive held over the counter. "I can crave what I want. So back off, sister." She plopped her money on the counter, grabbed a tissue from a box and greedily reached inside the bag for a piece of golden brittle. She took an exaggerated bite.

"You are crazy." Lynn laughed.

"Blissfully. That's the way God wants me to feel. I mean, goodness gracious—look how He's blessed me. I certainly don't deserve any of it, so I'm surely going to enjoy it like I'm supposed to."

"You have got to have the most optimistic mind of anyone I've ever met."

Lacy's electric-blue eyes settled on Lynn, seriousness overtaking mirth. "Oh, Lynn, after the year it took for me to conceive I'm just so grateful."

"It's hard to believe it was that long."

Lacy started to bite down on another piece of brittle but paused. "I was beginning to think I couldn't get pregnant but it was just God's timing. The man upstairs was just telling me to hold on to my horses till He gave me the go-ahead. And He taught me a big lesson in compassion and patience while I waited."

That was pure Lacy, always trying to figure out what God was trying to teach her. Lynn wasn't always so good at that.

"Well, I hate to run out on great company but I've got to go. Enjoy your time at home this afternoon."

Lacy grinned. "Will do and you, too. I hear you've got some handsome help coming over. Y'all have fun!"

Lynn stopped with her hand on the doorknob. "And how did you know that?"

"Little birdies told me. Well, big birdies, actually. Chance told Cole when he saw him this morning that he was helping you this afternoon. Cole told Seth and Wyatt, and it went like wildfire as soon as App and Stanley got wind of it. And yes, the posse knows, too."

Lynn let out a groan. "Great. Just great. Now everyone

will instantly jump to conclusions. I'm just letting the man help me build a tree house."

"Yep and I'm only eating one piece of this brittle. Relax. Enjoy and build a *great* tree house. Who knows where that will lead…. Lynn and Chance, sitting in a tree. First comes love and then comes—"

"I'm outta here." Lynn laughed despite herself and headed toward her car. She heard Lacy continue the song as the door closed behind her.

She glanced around and felt like she was sneaking out of town as she got into her car and drove down Main Street. The entire town knew Chance was coming out to her house again. And she knew exactly where it would lead. Straight to overblown hopes for love and romance, which wasn't happening. Yes, the man was gorgeous. Good to her boys and extremely useful around the house… Her ex-husband had been none of those things. So it really felt unfair to let her experience with her ex color her view of Chance. But she painted all men with that brush where she and her boys were concerned.

Where this was going? Nowhere. She'd just gotten carried away with her soft side, and Chance had looked so woebegone and sad last night that on a crazy impulse she'd hugged him. Hugged him for a pretty long time.

An extremely nice, long time. And now she knew…

No hugging allowed. None. Zero. Never again.

Chapter Ten

"If you'll hold this then I'll attach it," Chance said several hours later.

Lynn was crouched beside him, shoulder to shoulder, on the now sturdy floor of the tree house. They were using a cordless drill to attach the walls to the floor with screws. Below them the boys and Tiny ran in circles playing cowboys with their popguns. They were thrilled with the tree house.

"I would hope you know I would never have gotten this done without you. My boys would have probably hurt themselves in what I could have built them."

Chance pushed the power button and the screw ate through the wood in less than ten seconds. He sat back on his knees and let the drill rest on his thigh. "You were trying. That says something. And the best way to learn is to be taught. I'm a good teacher, if you haven't noticed." He gave a cocky grin and it did crazy fluttery things to her insides.

This was a glimpse of Chance Turner, relaxed and not being so hard on himself. Until that moment she hadn't realized exactly how difficult Randy's death had been for him.

But now she knew his unguarded side and realized that Chance Turner could be dangerous. She tried to look unaffected and casual. "You're a little cocky for a preacher, aren't you?" She laughed.

"Hey, God never said a preacher was supposed to be a passive, no-personality kind of guy."

She was hyperaware of where her jean-clad knee was touching his. "I guess you have a point."

"You're right, I do. Look at Peter. There was nothing about him that was passive. Passionate, yes. Passive—no way. Strong men can be Christians."

"Hey, you sound a little defensive," she teased, enjoying herself more than she could fathom. It was a beautiful, crisp winter day, the sun was sparkling, her children were playing and she was having an entertaining, enlightening conversation with a devastatingly handsome cowboy. It was lovely.

He crunched his straight black eyebrows. "Oh, believe me, there are some out there who think a preacher has to have a milkweed handshake and his chin to his chest. But God tells me and all His other kids to be bold. Courageous. Men of courage. Patient and kind, yes. But there is a balance." He paused. "I guess that could sound arrogant. Believe me, I'm not. The Lord has forgiven me a lot. I'm no better than the lowest sinner out there. None of us are. But I try to be the man God would want me to be." He took a deep breath and turned his head to the side, staring out at the cattle in the distance.

"You aren't preaching right now. Why is that?" she asked. "You are clearly called to it."

He was passionate. It was obvious now. But he was deeply caring and compassionate to have been so affected by one from his congregation. She guessed that was what Randy had been. Having church in an arena didn't change that.

Chance pulled himself back from wherever his thoughts had gone and reached for another board. "I don't have it in me. I just feel like my well is empty." He stood the board up and she grabbed it and held it like she'd done the other one. Their fingers brushed as hers replaced his, and the butterflies that had been dancing on and off all morning exploded into motion.

She tried to concentrate on what was being discussed and the importance of it and not this attraction she was feeling toward him. "When you talk just now you don't sound empty. You sound like a man with a lot to say and to offer. But I know what you mean. Not from a preacher's standpoint, but I know what you mean about feeling empty. I never thought about it exactly that way, but that's kind of how I feel about the thought of remarrying." Why was she going there? It had just come out. "I know everyone sees me and my boys and they think it would be so lovely for me to find a good man—a cowboy—and remarry and live happily ever after." She gave him an embarrassed smile. His eyes were serious and caring as he listened. "I've thought about it. But unlike Stacy, who is trying to get married, or Rose, who married Zane, I just don't think I have in me what it takes to be a wife again. I feel like I can be a good mother."

"You are a good mother. A great mother."

Her heart jumped at his soft words of reassurance. "Thank you. But as far as a wife, I feel like my well is dry, too." She was totally embarrassed. Waving her hand, she huffed, "Ignore all of that. It isn't anything at all like what you are feeling. I shouldn't have even tried to make a comparison. It probably makes no sense at all."

He set the drill down and grabbed her fluttering hand. "No. Stop. You make perfect sense. I don't know what all you went through, but you're a strong woman. I can tell that. You've come out on top here with your boys. No one can judge or even try to know someone else's heart. But God does know, and with time He'll heal even that dry well. One day you may be able to love again. Your time to heal is your own. No one else's."

He was rubbing his thumb across the back of her hand and his words comforted her…as did his touch. Lifting her chin, she looked into his eyes and felt an overwhelming sense of…assurance. He was good at what God had called him to do.

"Thank you," she said. "I was feeling some pressure from several sides."

"They mean well." He winked and gently laid her hand on her knee, patting the back of it once before picking up his drill again. It was almost as if he regretted letting her hand go.

She concentrated on placing the next board of the tree house in place. Her thoughts guiltily went to Stacy. She'd yet to ask him again to perform Stacy's wedding. Knowing what he was going through now, she was conflicted.

"So about you?" she said. She hadn't meant to sidetrack talking about him. "You were ministering to me just now. You do it naturally."

"Some things come naturally. That doesn't mean I'm not stuck on the sandbar in the middle of river. I'm sorry about your friend's wedding. I've been thinking about that ever since you asked me, but that's her special day and I just don't feel like I'm where I need to be to be involved in it."

Looking at him no one would guess Chance Turner would ever get stranded. "I wish you were. She—" Lynn stopped. This was about him right now. "And this has to do with Randy's death."

The pain instantly dulled his green eyes to a pale hue and his handsome features went slack with the weight of the burden he carried. Lynn's heart cracked seeing it. She leaned the board against the attached one and gave him her full attention. "Is it that you didn't realize he was on drugs?"

He took a deep breath, and let it out slowly through tense lips. "Funny how I can counsel and give advice and can't get it in my own head and mind."

A sharp stab of empathy sliced through Lynn. She got it. She understood exactly what he was saying. "I guess it's the eighteen-inch rule. Many people miss Heaven because of the eighteen inches between their brain and their heart. The two don't always connect." She started to say, *Believe me, I know,* but held back. She couldn't keep bringing the conversation to herself.

This was about Chance.

"I'm just taking time off, trying to find my way. Giving God time to pull me off the sandbar. Helping you and the boys is a good thing." He lifted the drill and pulled the trigger. Twice. "So put me to work," he said over the whirring roar.

"Okay, anything I can do."

"Momma, can we come up there yet?" Gavin skidded to a halt at the base of the ladder.

Jack was right behind him. "We ain't gonna fall." He grabbed hold of the ladder and jumped on the bottom rung.

"What do you think, boss lady?" Chance's eyes twinkled. "Do you feel safe enough to let them come up and maybe start helping build this thing?"

She looked around at the two sides that were finished. "If they stay on that side I won't worry so much that they'll try to jump from the floor to the ground."

"Nice way to not say they might fall."

She laughed. "Knowing those two, they would jump intentionally just to see if they could do it."

"Come on up, but careful," Chance called. Jack scooted up the ladder like a squirrel up a tree.

Chance took him by the arms and helped him onto the deck of the tree house. "Dude, I thought you said you were scared of climbing a ladder?"

Jack's face blew up with a radiant smile. "I'm not scared of *this*. I'm scared of *that*." He waved toward the house and the tall eaves. "That's e-*nor*-mous.

"It ain't enormous. Clint Matlock's barn, that's enormous," Gavin declared, hot on the heels of his brother. Chance reached for him also. "And I'm not scared of any of it." Gavin beamed, then looked at Lynn. "But I'm not gonna scare you again, Momma. Just like Chance told me."

He was scaring her all right, just by his big talk! "What did Chance tell you?" she asked, her curiosity spiked.

"That boys can be daredevils but cal-cu-lated. They got to be prepared and trained up for dangerous stuff so's it balances the scale. But sometimes they just gotta think about their mommas."

She laughed nervously. "Well, thank you for thinking of me. If you become a daredevil I'm going to grow old before my time."

"And she's too pretty to grow old before her time. Don't you boys agree?"

Chance had just called her pretty. The compliment was just to tease with her boys and yet there was no denying the way it washed over her. It had been a very long time since a man had told her she was pretty.

She didn't look at him. Instead she looked at her grinning boys.

Gavin spoke first. "We ain't gonna do that to you, Momma. Are we, Jack?"

Jack shook his head. He turned serious. "You think my momma is pretty?"

Chance hiked a straight black brow charmingly and showed his even more charming half grin. "I think you've got a beautiful mom inside and out."

Gavin and Jack stared at her with the excitement of two children who'd just won the Toys "R" Us lottery.

She laughed, self-conscious about the moment. "You don't really know me," she said, teasing but serious.

He looked shocked. "So you're telling me you aren't nice?"

"Oh, she's nice," Gavin said. "Except when we don't do what she says!"

"Oh, yeah." Jack giggled when she shot them a teasing scowl. "She makes us sit in time-out forever!"

She knew he was playing, getting into the spirit of things. She poked him in the rib and he jumped away squealing. Chance caught him around the waist and poked him, too, as Jack wrapped his arms around Chance's neck. "Your momma is just teaching you right from wrong because she loves you."

"We know," Gavin said, launching himself toward Chance, wanting to be included in the hug. Lynn's heart caught—partly because they were up so high and partly because of how hungry her boys were for male affection.

Laughing, Chance caught him and pulled him close, keeping him safe.

Lynn took in the sweet picture. It sent an ache of longing through her like nothing she'd experienced…. Her boys were on the safe side of the tree house with Chance in between them and the edge. Looking at them, it was easy to see what they were missing. Her boys were missing the man in their life who was supposed to love them and protect them from the hard, dangerous things in life.

Her boys were missing that because she thought she was enough for them.

But was she?

Meeting Chance's eyes, she smiled back at him and tried to enjoy the moment and not make more of this than she should.

She and her boys were doing great. And if she looked at it from Chance's point of view, this was good for him, too. This moment was a way to relieve some of the strain he was feeling from Randy's death. That's what this was. A great moment for her boys and for Chance.

She didn't need to complicate it with all this other stuff suddenly rolling around in her head. Like the realization that Chance Turner was a man she could trust. He was a man she could trust with all the shattered pieces hidden inside her heart.

A shattered piece of glass wasn't fixable. There were too many pieces crushed to dust particles that were irreparable. It was the same with her heart. Some women at the shelter with worse stories than hers were moving on. Stacy was one of them. But as hard as she'd tried to encourage others to take the step, she'd realized that her heart was too shattered. She couldn't and wouldn't put herself through believing in someone again.

But seeing her boys with Chance told her that they were going to suffer in the long run because she couldn't let go of her past.

Chance was wrong. She wasn't pretty on the inside or she'd be able to forgive and forget and move on.

Her ex had been manipulative and mind controlling. And though she'd finally gotten out, it was a struggle. She'd come to realize deep in her heart that he still controlled her, even though she hadn't seen or talked to him in over three years. It made her feel weak.

She didn't like knowing this about herself, but as much as she tried she couldn't get past it. Some people could trust again. She couldn't. And it seemed nothing or no one could change that.

Chapter Eleven

Lynn pulled herself out of the dumps by the next morning and headed over to the shelter. Dottie had called and asked her to talk to a new resident, Sandra, who she thought Lynn could help. Though Lynn was able to help others, she often felt like a hypocrite because she still had her own hang-ups. But she never refused to share her experience or to listen to a new resident pour out her heartache. Lynn never omitted that she still had struggles—a hang-up where trust was concerned.

When it came to trust, each person had to work that out on her own timetable. It was much like grief. One person's time to grieve the loss of a loved one was not charted on the same schedule as someone else.

She did know and recognize that God had brought her through and she had a great life! She *did*.

Sandra was a nervous wreck. She was a small woman with a kind face that wore the bright purple marks of a fresh beating and a swollen eye full of blood. In her eyes, behind everything, Lynn saw the struggle. She'd seen this over and over again and every time it made her sick to her stomach. But unlike the way she'd almost lost it at the bachelor auction, here she always was able to hold on to her emotions. When she was talking to women like Sandra it was all about helping free them.

Dottie, tall and willowy with a slight limp left over from a near fatal meeting with a hurricane, had hugged Lynn the minute she arrived, and had introduced her to Sandra. Dottie was a Godsend for the shelter. They stood in an awkward moment as the boys raced each other to the large swing set the men of Mule Hollow had built them. A little girl sat on a swing hugging her doll.

"This is Margaret," Dottie said. "She's seven and loves babies."

"Hi, Margaret, it's good to meet you," Lynn said. She never asked a child how she was doing when she'd just arrived. Poor children were disoriented, afraid, usually confused and scared. But putting that into words right off the bat to a total stranger was hard. Lynn knew from her own boys' experience that it was best to let them acclimate slowly. Margaret didn't say anything, just hugged her doll closer and looked at her mother. Lynn's heart went out to the child, just for having to look into her mother's bruised and swollen face.

Overwhelmed with compassion and the desire to help, Lynn smiled at Sandra. "Let's go talk. If you want to?"

Sandra nodded.

"I'll watch the children." Dottie patted her five-month-old's padded bottom. "You take all the time you need. Margaret can help me babysit. How does that sound?" Dottie held her hand out to Margaret. The little girl glanced at her mother. Sandra nodded and Margaret reached out and took Dottie's hand.

Lynn led the way to the parlor that they used for group sessions and one-on-one meetings. Brady's parents had dreamed of having a huge family and had built this giant ranch home in anticipation. But God hadn't had it in His plan and they'd only been blessed late in life with Brady. Brady had turned the house into No Place Like Home. And this parlor, which had been used little in the years before the shelter, had become a room where much heartache was shared and much healing begun. Brady loved to say that his parents had had a dream for the house, but God had had a bigger dream.

As she led Sandra into the pretty pale blue room, Lynn prayed that she could be God's facilitator of the beginning of Sandra's healing process.

To her surprise she didn't have to coax anything out of Sandra. She was ready to speak. Ready to try and find answers. Like Lynn had been when she'd finally left her husband, Sandra was seeking a way to stop the cycle. She was just trying to get her mind around how to do it. She opened up and everything flooded out…. She was so upset that trust wasn't an issue. She just needed someone. And she was worried that her abuse was her fault.

"No, Sandra, it's not your fault. You can't think about how long you stayed. You're out now," Lynn said, not too long into the conversation. "From this point on you have to look forward. God led me out of my abusive marriage, but I did the same thing as you. I let myself stay in that situation far longer than I should have. I was mixed up and I'd heard so many lies, and so many situations had been twisted, and over time I was turned inside out and unable to see clearly. Distance helps us see more clearly. Each passing day helps…. There may be emotional scars that take far longer to heal than those marks on your face. But life can be better for you and Margaret. I promise."

Sandra wrung her hands together in her lap. "But my mother despises that I've done this. She says that God hates divorce and that I'll reap the consequences of my actions for the rest of my life."

Good, well-meaning—and not so well-meaning— Christian folks could be so judgmental, so clueless sometimes. "You were living in a dangerous situation for you and your child. Yes, God wants marriages to last, but I don't believe God wants us to stay in a situation like that. I have to answer for leaving my marriage one day and, Sandra, I am proud to say that I kept my boys safe. You and I both have no one to be accountable to for our action except God."

Sandra contemplated that before nodding. "I understand."

"No one understands like those of us who have been down this road. For me, leaving was hard to do. Despite the pain and the fear I lived with and as unhealthy as my situation was, it was still hard to make myself leave." Drew had hit her during his drunken, emotional rages, and his infidelities, followed by contrite apologies, were always the same. And always painful.

She finally realized they were merely his way of manipulating her into doing exactly what he wanted her to do—abusive in so many ways.

"But maybe I could have done something different," Sandra said. "Margaret loves her daddy."

"It's not your fault, no matter what, when a man hits you."

Drew had always managed to make it Lynn's fault. Toward the end he'd grown more and more physically abusive, as if the more he hit her the easier it was. And she'd allowed it, believing the lie that somehow it was her fault. "We do things we shouldn't because we love our spouses—so we put up with things and believe the one we love when he says it's our fault. Sandra, God gave you Margaret to love and protect. You have taken the first step toward doing just that."

Lynn totally understood where Sandra was coming from. She'd started out as a strong person but somehow she'd lost her way. At some point her mind told her this was the way she was supposed to live. And the way it had happened…she'd lost herself and her path because of the worst part—how much she'd loved Drew and trusted him.

She was so ashamed to admit to herself or anyone that she'd loved a man who could do that to her. If it hadn't been for her boys she would have stayed there. It was humiliating to realize that about herself. With distance she'd understood that any love she'd ever had for Drew had been wiped out by the bad things he'd done. And that gave her freedom. But the issue remained that she'd misjudged him and loved him in the first place. How, how, she asked herself, had she ever loved a man like that? Was her judgment that bad?

She and Sandra talked for over an hour and Sandra seemed to feel better and stronger about what she'd done when they finished. A long road lay ahead, but at least Sandra was on the path to freedom and healing.

Lynn hoped she'd helped Sandra. But she was thinking about herself as she drove away. She would never allow herself to become embroiled in a bad marriage again. She feared it more than anything in life. It would not happen. God had helped her over the last few years to know what a great life she had now. And to believe that she and her boys would and could be okay. It was just that lately niggling doubts and worries had started in on her. Why now, when everything was going so well?

Chance's tires crushed the gravel of Lynn's drive as he pulled to a stop. It had rained but he'd noticed Lynn didn't have a Christmas tree. So what did he do? He asked her if he could take her and the boys to cut one. He'd come over two straight days and worked on the tree house and it was now finished. He could have disappeared and gone out to the stagecoach house for the solitude he needed, but the boys really wanted a tree.

He'd picked up some wood to repair Lynn's front porch. Lifting the lumber from the truck, he carried it around the back of the house to the barn. Tiny sloshed around in the mud, dashing all around Chance, and before he made it to the back door it flew open and the boys raced out. They wore rubber boots and coats that could repel the wet, cold weather. He felt good seeing them.

"Hey, buckaroos!"

"Merry Christmas, Chance," Gavin yelled, jumping in a puddle.

"No, Gavin," Jack exclaimed. "Momma said don't get wet. We're goin' ta get a tree. Now."

"Gavin," Lynn said, coming to a halt on the back step. "Your brother is right. What did I tell you?"

Chance hid a laugh as Gavin reluctantly stepped out of the puddle and looked up at his mother.

"Don't get wet," Gavin said. "I'll be too cold to go get a tree."

The kid was funny. "Then load up," Chance said. "Let's get us a tree."

The boys whooped and raced off around the corner, sloshing through shallow puddles as they went.

"Hi." Lynn sighed. "All I can do is try."

Chance instinctively gave her a one-armed hug as he met her twinkling eyes. "It's all good."

"Yes it is." She looked up at him. "Are you ready for this?"

His heart felt as if it were being pumped up like a balloon. Goodness, she took his breath away. "I was born ready."

But looking at her, holding her close and wanting to hold her closer, he knew he wasn't ready at all.

Chapter Twelve

Lynn walked beside Chance as they followed the boys through the woods on the Turner ranch. Her thoughts were distracted. When Chance had put one arm around her and looked into her eyes her world had begun to spin. She'd been thinking about him before he got there. Ever since he'd played with her boys in that tree house, she'd been thinking about it—how her boys were on the safe side, with Chance in between them and the edge. It had been so easy to see what they were missing. So easy to see what they could have if she were able to fall in love with a good man. Because she knew in that moment in that unfinished tree house, with two sides built and two sides open, that her boys missed having a man in their life to love and protect them.

Walking beside Chance, looking for a Christmas tree, underlined the fact in bold black.

Her boys were missing that because she thought she was enough for them.

But was she? No.

She'd looked into Chance's eyes and wanted him to embrace her like a man in love would do. She'd wanted him to kiss her…wanted to feel cherished and protected. She'd looked into Chance's eyes and wanted her life to be different. Wanted all the horrible past to have never happened. If it had never happened then there was hope for her—but she wouldn't have her boys. She closed her eyes and sighed, feeling the strength of Chance's embrace. Her past had happened and nothing could make it not so. Her boys were the proof that God could make good from any bad situation. She wouldn't choose a clear past over her sons.

And she and her boys were doing great. That was what she told herself when she'd stepped out of Chance's embrace. It was what she told herself as she'd pretended his touch hadn't affected her.

But it had.

"What about this one?" Gavin yelled. He was standing beside a gigantic cedar tree.

"I think that's a little too big," Chance called. He was walking beside her as Jack and Gavin bounded from one tree to the next.

"You sure are quiet," he said.

"Sorry."

"Is it something I did?"

"No. It's just stuff."

"Can I help?"

No, he couldn't, because the stuff she was dealing with was knowing Chance Turner was a trustworthy man. He was a man she could trust with all the shattered pieces hidden inside her heart. And yet she couldn't do it. She thought of Sandra and all she'd told her…. She prayed that, like so many of the others, Sandra could become totally free from her past.

Lynn hated admitting that she wasn't free from her own past. Hated admitting that she was more fragile than she wanted to be. But it was true. She wasn't just cracked, she was broken on an emotional level.

"What is bothering you?"

She sighed and was glad for the cold air on her hot cheeks. "My ex was a manipulative man. And though I finally got out, it's been, and still is a struggle. I'm dealing with issues this morning."

His expression was understanding. And yet she knew he couldn't understand.

"I hope you know you can trust me," Chance said, as if he'd been reading her mind.

She stopped walking and studied a cedar. It was too small but it gave her something to concentrate on. "I have a hard time trusting men."

"I know. But I still hope you'll realize you can trust me."

"My boys are crazy about you. I guess you've figured that out."

His lips twisted in that pulse-igniting grin of his. "I don't know what I did to garner that honor but I like it."

"Kids are good judges of character."

"How about you?"

"Sometimes," she said, wishing she could say yes, but it wouldn't be true. "I misjudged Drew in the worst possible way and, though I no longer bear the physical signs of that mistake, psychologically I still have issues."

"Do you want to talk about it?"

She pulled her knitted scarf closer around her neck

and shook her head. The kids were squealing in the woods ahead and that was where she wanted to be…not here, where she suddenly wanted more than anything to feel Chance's arms tightly around her. To feel the beat of his heart against her ear. How could she want that so deeply and still be scared to death of him?

She hated this. "You know what—enough." She inhaled and smiled like she meant it. "We came to find a tree and have a good time and that is what I want to be doing." She headed toward the laughter ringing through the trees. She was going to have fun and not think about all the dirt from her past. "Today is a great day," she said, her confidence building.

"Yes, it is. You're a brave woman, Lynn. A strong woman. I'm the first to tell you that I'm having issues of my own, which you are well aware of, so I completely understand what you're saying."

"I know. It's crazy, isn't it. I know God has gotten me to this point and it's fantastic, considering where I was. Why then can't I get past this moment?"

"Hey, look around at this beautiful place and listen to your children laughing." He took her hand. "This is a good moment." He paused, looking up at the treetops while the sound of her children's laughter echoed on the chilly air, and then he smiled at her. "Let's just think about this moment right now."

He was right. It sounded like a good plan.

Planting a smile on her face and in her heart on Saturday morning, Lynn headed to the church. She had to drop by the feed store and pick up some dog food first, and they ran into App and Stanley buying their weekly bag of sunflower seeds. While she paid for the dog food the two older men and her boys went outside. She watched through the window as they stood on the sidewalk and practiced their sunflower spitting. Boys would be boys no matter what ages.

As soon as she herded Gavin and Jack into the car they began copying the way App and Stanley talked. It never failed after being around them. Thankfully, it *usually* lasted only a few days before they went back to their normal vernacular.

"I ate me some *sunflours,* Momma," Jack drawled.

"Yup," Gavin said. "Them thar thangs is the best ta spit."

She bit her tongue and concentrated on getting to the church. It was less than three weeks till Christmas and practice was starting on the children's Christmas pageant. Like everything else around here, it had been started as a way to get women to come to Mule Hollow. Not just as a matchmaking endeavor but also as a witness with the story of Jesus' birth. Lacy had been in charge and she was always excited about spreading the good news and witnessing to everyone about God's ability to save and redeem. But this year she was due to deliver close to Christmas and had been unable to take charge. It just seemed that one thing after the other had kept folks from stepping up. The Barn Theater, started by Ross and Sugar Ray Denton, was having a Christmas-themed program involving several resident cowboys and cowgirls and so it really didn't seem necessary to have a community pageant. Lynn and several ladies had decided that the children needed a program and so Lynn had volunteered to head that up.

The last person she expected to see when she pulled into the church parking lot was Chance.

"Look, it's Chance!" the boys squealed in unison. They were crazy about the man. Crazy about him.

He was leaning against his pickup with his boots crossed at the ankles, his hat hunkered down low over his eyes against the sparkling winter sunlight. Involuntarily her stomach dropped and she smiled like a schoolgirl, which she certainly was not!

He nudged his hat back and grinned, coming to place his hand on her open door. "I guess I got the time wrong. I showed up thirty minutes ago."

"What are you doing here?"

"We invited him," Gavin boasted, jumping out of the backseat. He tilted his head all the way back and grinned up at Chance. "We didn't thank you was actually going to come though."

Jack jumped from the car. "We shor nuff didn't," he said, in his App-and-Stanley slang. Okay, so she might have to talk to the boys about copying everything the two older men said.

"Didn't you two tell me your mom needed help?"

Their eyes grew wide as saucers. Gavin spoke first. "You're not s'posed to tell her that."

"Why did you tell him that in the first place?"

Jack looked shocked. "But you said you did."

"I didn't mean—" She got out of the car, where she really felt hemmed-in looking up at Chance from her seat. "Do you really want to help?

He glanced toward the white church. "I do."

The man confused her. He didn't want to preach right now, he was struggling spiritually and yet he was volunteering to help with the children's ministry.... It suddenly hit her that maybe this wasn't about her, but was about Chance. Maybe God was using all this for him. Once more she bit her lip and she prayed she'd stop thinking about her own situation and focus on his. Maybe God was going to use this to help Chance refill his well. It wasn't hard to see what a wonderful man he was. Though he was hurting inside, he was still reaching out to help her and now the children.

"Sure. That's great. Follow me to the sanctuary. Boys, do not, and I repeat, do not barrel around the corners of this church and slam into anyone. You may go play on the swing set until everyone starts to arrive but slow down around corners." The ground had dried up since the morning's rain but it was still moist in places. Although thankfully here at the church there hadn't been anything more than a drizzle. Mud and kids and a church were not a good combination.

"We'll try, Momma," Gavin said with a heavy sigh, as if trying to control his speed was the largest weight he could possibly bear. Jack had already raced off toward the back of the church.

"*Jack Robert Perry,* did you hear me?" she called in her sternest voice. The little tyke put the brakes on instantly and turned to look at her innocently. Right.

"I wasn't gonna run when I was coming back."

"Don't run going either."

"Okay, Momma. But little boys are supposed to run, don't you know that?"

She cleared her throat trying to hold back a grin. "Yes, I do know that, but they are also supposed to mind their mommas."

"Yes, ma'am," Jack said as Gavin reached him. They headed off together at a snail's pace, overemphasizing their dragging feet.

Chance chuckled watching them disappear around the corner. "You sound pretty mean there."

"Ha! I sound like a mother."

"That you do. You have a good poker face, too."

She gave him a look of shock. "You noticed that? And here I thought I was fooling everyone."

"Yeah, right. They turn you to mush, and me and anyone watching for two seconds can see it."

She pulled two bags of refreshments from the backseat. "I didn't think I was that transparent."

Chance reached for the bags. "Here, let me take that. And I'm just teasing you."

"You had better watch your step since we are about to be bombarded with ten kids—none over the age of eight—for this dress rehearsal."

"Sounds like fun." He fell into step with her, then waited at the front door as she inserted the key and opened the big oak door. "I'll be sure and look around all corners. So, what's the program?"

"It's the Christmas story from the shepherd's point of view. We wanted to have it be from the donkey's point of view and use Samantha—you know, Cort and Lilly Wells's cute donkey."

"Oh, yeah, I've heard about that donkey's shenanigans."

"The kids love that little donkey but we decided bringing Samantha into the sanctuary was not a good idea."

He cocked a brow. "Nope, not a good idea."

They laughed as she flipped on the light switch and then led the way down to the front of the quaint church.

The sun was filtering in through the stained glass, glinted off the dark wooden pews and made patchworks along the planked floor. "I love this sanctuary," she said, feeling the warmth of the place and the serenity. "There is just a sense of peace that overcomes me when I walk inside. As much as I love Samantha, her clomping down the aisle wouldn't be appropriate."

"I agree. On all counts. I can still remember my first time to come here to worship. I accepted Jesus as my savior right here in this very spot." He'd come to stand in front of the pulpit and was staring thoughtfully at it.

"Then this is a special place on a personal level to you. I think that's great. I want my boys to experience that when the Lord leads them to make a commitment. It's just so wonderful to have roots in the Lord."

And it was. "It means so much to me that my boys have roots. All the women at the shelter feel the same way." She paused and then couldn't stop herself from continuing. "That's what Stacy wants for her wedding. She is such a sweetheart, Chance. She's been through so much in her life and she has been so horribly mistreated by every man in her life...and yet she has a quiet spirit of survival. And she has found a dedicated, loving Christian man she is brave enough to marry—despite all the abuse she's lived through with her dad and former husband. You called me brave. *That* is a brave woman."

"Sounds like it."

"She would never believe that, but she is. And this

wedding means so much to her. Finding a preacher to perform the ceremony who is connected to them is very important to her."

"What about Brady?"

"He and Dottie have been lifesavers to her and she could easily have him do the wedding. But she wants a man of God performing the ceremony. She wants to stand here, where we are in this church sanctuary, and say her vows before God and all of her new Mule Hollow family."

Chance looked thoughtful and she wondered what he was thinking. She wanted to come right out and ask him again to do the wedding but something inside her held her back. He was waging his own spiritual battle inside his heart and soul and he didn't need pressure from her. God would lead him as he was ready.

Chapter Thirteen

"No, Wes, you carry it this way. Hold it up."

Chance stood to the side of the little troupe of children lined up at the front of the church. He was totally engaged in watching Gavin show the smaller boy, Wes McKennon, how to hold his staff in his pudgy hand. The dark-haired little boy was trying very hard to do what he was supposed to do.

"Gavin, you're doing a great job helping Wes." Chance bent on one knee, deciding he could help the tot hold the staff the correct way. "And you're doing a good job holding this staff, Wes." Chance knew the boy could hold the staff upside down or sideways and the audience was going to think he was fantastic no matter what he did. As for Gavin, rattling off instructions—the kid was born to be an organizer and leader. The boy was full of instructions for everyone and the other kids were listening when he spoke.

And not just kids. Chance still couldn't believe he himself was here. Gavin also had the gift of persuasion where adults were concerned—or at least where Chance was. Gavin had asked him to help with the program and Chance had come. And he was enjoying himself. He'd also had fun cutting down the Christmas tree and helping the boys with the lights and the tree house.

"Okay, boys and girls, let's stand up straight and sing so the people on the back pew will hear you. You are doing a great job."

Jack was standing beside a toddler who was sucking his thumb and taking everything in with gigantic eyes. This was Stacy's baby. She was with the other mothers decorating the annex for lunch after the sermon and the program. The Mule Hollow Church of Faith was a busy church. He watched Lynn working with the kids. She'd said she wanted roots for her boys. As a cowboy preacher he hadn't really set any roots down for himself. He stayed on the road much of the time. When he wasn't at a rodeo he was at an auction barn or a roping or any manner of other places where he was called or invited. But that was where his heart was. That was where God had put him.

One lost soul. Randy. Why hadn't he been able to lead Randy to the Lord? Why hadn't he seen that Randy had a problem.… If he considered Randy his flock then why hadn't he recognized that he was in trouble? That torment had a grip on him that he couldn't ease. Why hadn't God given him the time to help Randy physically and spiritually?

"Mr. Turner, could I speak to you?"

The soft voice drew him from the fog of his internal debate and he turned around. Stacy was sitting on the pew behind him looking pensive.

"Sure," he said, wanting instantly to ease her discomfort. "Outside?"

He nodded, glanced at the group of kids and Lynn as she led them in a song, then got up and followed Stacy. Lynn had told her that Stacy had a hard time trusting men. That she'd come a long way, thanks to some very special men in Mule Hollow who'd been kind and set good, godly examples for her of how real men should behave. On the porch she faced him. Her pale blond hair was pulled back in a clasp, totally exposing her fine, dainty features. She was beautiful in an almost angelic sense—the perfect choice for a Christmas angel. Sky-blue eyes, kind with a wariness that still could not be hidden, despite the kindness she'd been shown here in Mule Hollow. Just looking at her and knowing some of her story, he wanted only the best for her.

"What can I do for you?" he asked, trying to put her at ease, pretty certain he knew what she wanted.

"Lynn, I'm sure, asked you to perform my and Emmett's wedding ceremony. I know you aren't preaching right now, if I understand that correctly, but I was just hoping that I could ask you to please consider it once more." Tears welled in her eyes but she blinked and they disappeared in an instant. He got the feeling she didn't usually speak a whole lot. "I—I've decided I want to get married next Saturday." She glanced at the ground then, almost as if forcing herself, she met his gaze again. "I've been dragging my feet, coming up with all kinds of excuses for why now isn't the time to marry Emmett— there isn't a preacher I want, I'm afraid, I could be hurt again." She breathed in hard. "But I know it's wrong. I love Emmett and he loves me…." She softly cleared her throat. Probably for courage to push onward—it was clear in her eyes how hard this was for her. "So, I had to ask you personally if you might marry us next Saturday."

Chance's heart cracked, remembering everything Lynn had told him about Stacy. God help him, there was no way he could tell her no. What kind of man would he be to do that? Meeting her sincere gaze with one of assurance he said, "I would be honored."

"Chance, are you out here?"

Chance was repairing a broken slat on one of the old stalls in the stagecoach house's barn. He straightened and called, "I'm here," stepping out where Lynn could see him.

"You left without a word," she said as she saw him and strode toward him. "And then Stacy told me that you'd agreed to marry them next week and I couldn't believe it. I'm so excited! But, are you all right with that?"

He had been asking himself the same question for the last hour. "I guess I have to be. After she pushed herself to get the courage up to ask me to do it, how could I say no? Who could say no to someone as gentle and kind-looking as Stacy?"

"Oh, so you're saying I'm not sweet enough? That's why you so easily told me no?" Lynn crossed her arms and gave him an assessing look.

"No...I mean..." He stumbled over his words, realizing how that had sounded to her. "I'm sorry. That's not what I meant."

"Relax, I'm just teasing. I know what you mean."

She was laughing but he shook his head. "No. You're

just as sweet, Lynn. I just didn't get it until you'd told me her story and then I met her."

A pale tinge of pink touched her cheeks and her eyes softened. "No. I'm not—"

"Yes, you are." He touched her arm then, realizing Lynn's background might mean she wasn't used to compliments.

She studied his hand on her arm then raised her gaze to his. "It seems that God isn't playing fair with you."

He scowled. "You probably think I'm not worth much, pulling back like I have."

"No. I think you are a man grief-stricken for a lost soul. Maybe a little angry at God about it, and that has wiped you out inside. I've been thinking about that dry well you were talking about, and I think God's real busy trying to fill it up for you."

His scowl dug in deeper and he went back to the stall. Grabbing another nail, he bent to retrieve his hammer and sank the nail into the hardwood with two strikes.

"Impressive," Lynn said, leaning against the top plank and looking down at him. She'd been happy about Stacy, but deep inside it was costing him. His soul did ache. It was easy to tell. "Nothing like a hammer and nails to vent with," she said, feeling led to see if he needed to talk. It didn't go unnoticed that he wasn't using his cordless drill and wood screws.

"You are enjoying this."

"No. I'm sorry. I really think taking your frustrations out with hard work is very constructive. You get to vent, think about it, pray about it, accomplish something constructive at the same time. Believe you me, I can do some heavy-duty housecleaning when I'm mad as a hornet. I buzz around, hotter than fire, and my house sparkles like Mr. Clean himself has been to visit. I just recognized the tendency."

He stood up and hooked the hammer on the wooden slat. "So you probably thought me running out on you like that was pretty pathetic."

"So, you did run out on me. I looked around and you weren't there. It wasn't until Stacy came and told me the news that I thought—well, I wondered if you were okay."

He nodded. "I'm okay. God's working with me."

She really liked that about him. He was angry at God for not giving him the opportunity to lead Randy to the Lord. Angry at God for taking Randy before he had time to get straightened out. And yet he was waiting and letting God work on him.

"Thanks for coming to check on me."

His quiet words washed over her like the touch of a whispery breeze. "You're welcome." He smiled and she felt almost faint, her heart was pounding so fast. "I'm just so pleased you agreed to do this for Stacy and Emmett." She needed to get to a subject that wasn't attached to her emotions. Maybe that was what was wrong with her suddenly. She looked around the interior of the barn, trying not to think about how his gaze had seemed to touch something deep in the dark corner of her heart…. "This place is really old, isn't it? Am I wrong, or would this have been the same barn they used all those years ago to stable the stagecoach horses?"

"It is. We try to keep it in as good condition as possible. For over a hundred and fifty years old it still looks pretty good, don't you think?" The stable was a low-slung building but the ceiling was steep in the center and high enough to house the stagecoaches if needed. Then the roofline sloped low on both sides where the horse stables were. It wasn't used much anymore but Chance liked it. He enjoyed the relics left from days gone by, like the old horseshoes that were nailed along the top stable board running the length of the barn.

"Are these horseshoes from back then?"

"Yes," he said, pleased. "I wonder where those shoes have been?"

"It is a really neat thing, this history your family has here. Melody talks about it all the time."

Melody had met Seth because she was researching Sam Bass, the famous Texas outlaw. As a history teacher she was intrigued by the ranch and its past, and Wyatt had hired her to research their whole family. She'd done a great job and in the process married Seth.

"I love the stability of your family."

He placed his boot against the stall rung and leaned his back against the stall. "Oh, we have our share of dysfunction. No family doesn't."

"Yes, I know. But you have to remember all that I've seen. I really cannot express to you what this means to Stacy for you to marry them. It is like a blessing from God. And being able to take her children and grandchildren to the church one day and show them where it all started—that means so much to someone like Stacy. I know I sound like a broken record. But it is true. I pray that God will give you peace about it."

"Where are your kids?"

"They went with Lilly Wells to play with Joshua.

They just love going out there as much as they love going over to Susan's."

"So you have the evening free?" What was he doing?

"Well, I hadn't really thought about it but, yes, I guess I do. I—"

"Would you like to ride into Ranger and have dinner with me?"

"Like a date?"

Her startled question flew back at him almost before he could register that he'd actually asked her out. Sure, he asked ladies out but not when he knew they weren't interested. But he enjoyed her company and he needed to eat.

"Um, if you want to call it that. I just need to eat." It was a lame attempt to make it no big deal. She was looking at him with shining eyes, almost black in the filtered light of the barn. And it hit him looking at her that he really wanted her to say yes.

She stepped away from him and shook her head. "No. Thank you though. But I, I don't d—I mean, I ought to go home and catch up on my washing. And tomorrow is the play and, well, I just came out here to thank you for consenting to do Stacy's ceremony—"

"Okay, halt." He gave the time-out sign with his hands and pushed away from the fence. "You are choosing washing over dinner?"

She shook her head. "I told you I don't date."

He knew it so why did it suddenly irritate him? "This is to celebrate me doing the ceremony. How about that?"

"That's not really fair, you know."

He held up his hands. "Hey, no strings attached and besides, you yourself said that God wasn't really playing fair with me and you're right. So I'd say if He can do it then I can do it."

"That's pretty arrogant, if you ask me."

"Yup." What was he doing? *Enjoying her company, that's what.* "So what will it be?"

Chapter Fourteen

What was she doing? Sure, she'd not technically agreed to make it a date. She needed to run by one of the large superstores that were open late and pick up some gold pipe-cleaners to make the angel a halo. She'd decided just last week not to put a halo on the angel, but an angel needs a halo and that was that.

In the process she did need to eat. A quick call to Lilly confirmed that she could keep the boys later than they'd planned originally. The fact that Lilly sounded too excited when she'd learned that Chance was giving Lynn a ride to the store in Ranger was to be expected. After all, everyone else would believe from appearance that it was in fact a date. When it wasn't.

Lynn stared into her closet of clothes. She'd stopped thinking about dressing up a long time ago—not that she was considering it now. But really, if there was a dressy occasion, she had nothing appropriate.

She bit her lip and tugged a red sweater from a hanger. And a pair of black pants…she'd gotten both pieces of clothing three years ago when she'd arrived at the shelter. There was a large room there with all kinds of donated clothes. She took a deep breath to still the queasy feeling attacking her, and changed with no second-guessing. She would just have to do.

She was applying a touch of mascara when she heard the rumble of Chance's truck. He was early! Her nerves kicked up in panic and she jabbed herself in the eye with the mascara wand when she heard his truck door slam. Wet mascara smeared below her eyes in a sudden blinking fit and she stared at herself in the mirror. Grabbing a tissue, she scrubbed at her eyes.

She was in a mess. Rushing to the window she peeked through the curtain and saw him as he strode toward the front door. The man had dressed up. He was starched and ironed and spiffed up from one end of his shined-up boots to the top of his cream-colored Stetson!

And he looked good.

"Who are you trying to kid, the man looks great," she growled as she struggled to get the black mascara off. The doorbell chimed brightly and she felt like she was going to be sick! This was a date.

She didn't date.

It had been almost eight years since she'd gone on her last date, and look how that had turned out.

"Calm down. Deep breaths," she told herself. "Your last date wasn't so hot but you got Gavin and Jack out of the deal." Some semblance of calm came over her. At least she wasn't going to throw up and her knees weren't about to give out on her. "You aren't marrying the man. You are going to the superstore and to dinner. Period."

The fact that he looked gorgeous was merely a benefit of the evening.

Still, there was no denying as she went to answer the door that something about Chance Turner told her she needed to be careful. It might have been the fact that the sick feeling in her stomach had somehow turned to anticipation…. Tugging the door open she tried to appear calm. Cool. Collected.

What a joke.

All it took was that totally mischievous, slow smile and his gaze sweeping down her and back up to let her understand exactly how ridiculous it was—she was not collected, cool or calm. More like nervous, insecure, scared.

"Might I say you are looking lovely tonight," he drawled, tilting his head slightly, his eyes teasing.

And that was all it took. She laughed, so taken by surprise. "You may say it," she said, smiling like a fool. "I have to say I've never had that line used on me before."

"But it's not a line."

She pulled the door closed, feeling relaxed somewhat by his teasing. She couldn't tell him that he'd come up with the perfect way of putting a woman at ease.

Chance had almost panicked, he was so nervous about this date. *It's not a date,* he reminded himself. He'd repeated the phrase the entire time he was getting ready.

She agreed, too. Lynn had made every effort to convince him it was not a date.

He wasn't so sure now. It felt like a date as he'd walked up to her door. His nerves were rattled as he'd pressed the doorbell. Those nerves hadn't gone away when she'd come to the door, and they hadn't calmed down as they drove toward Ranger.

He was taking Lynn Perry to dinner. He was extremely thankful for gold pipe-cleaners and angel halos. "You're great with the kids," he said, after they'd exhausted all other small talk and driven a couple of miles in silence. "They seem ready for tomorrow."

"Thank you. But I didn't do all the work. They've been practicing those songs and the Bible verses in Sunday school for weeks now. Adela and Esther Mae made the costumes while Norma Sue gave them moral support."

He laughed, concentrating on keeping his eyes on the road. "I gather Norma Sue isn't a seamstress."

"You know, she can fix a host of things—tractors, toasters, the projector if it messed up—but put a needle in her hands and she becomes all thumbs."

"So why weren't any of them there today?"

"I think they were matchmaking. They realized you were going to be there," she said, with a shrug. "What can I say?"

"You know, now that I think about it, I saw Norma Sue's truck pass by while I was waiting on you." He went back to watching the road.

"The sneak."

He laughed. "Wouldn't they have a field day if they knew I was taking you to pick up supplies?"

When Chance came home for some solitude to deal with Randy's death, he hadn't anticipated being set up by the matchmakers...not that they'd been set up. Lynn being in his truck had nothing to do with anyone else but them.

Marriage and settling down wasn't something he really thought about. He'd assumed that one day he probably would, but he'd loved his life, loved his calling. He'd been happy.

"So what would you like to eat?" he asked, refocusing his thoughts. "Steak, Mexican, Italian?"

"Oh, I'm fine with anything."

"Hey, it's the lady's choice tonight. What would you like?" He winked. "I know you have to have an opinion."

She was silent and when he looked her way she was frowning.

"Lynn, it's not hard. I'd just like to take you somewhere you'd like to eat."

"Sorry. I, well, I'd really like Italian, if that's okay?"

That sounded really odd to him. "Sure, if the lady likes Italian then the lady gets Italian."

She smiled then, a sweet, somewhat sad smile that had him wondering what he'd said to cause that look.

Lynn's heart was doing odd things and all because Chance had genuinely wanted to take her somewhere she wanted to eat. It was nice. Touching, actually, and it made her momentarily sad to remember how her ex-husband had chosen everything. Chance acted like he knew Ranger well, drove straight to a building with an aged-looking sign and whipped into the parking lot.

"I haven't been here in a long time but if my memory serves me well—which is debatable—they have great food." He hopped from the truck and by the time she had her seat belt off he was opening her door!

"What's wrong?" he asked as he held out his hand.

She was staring, she knew, and making all kinds of a fool out of herself, but this was too much. She'd seen several of the cowboys around town open a truck door for their girlfriends and wives and it always sent a shiver of envy through her. She'd never had that…until tonight. Chance Turner was not only generous in spirit and with his time, his smiles and his talents, he was also a gentleman. "Nothing's wrong," she said, taking the hand he offered her. "I'm just not used to the cowboy way."

She'd spoken as she stepped down from the truck and instead of him stepping back as she'd expected, he planted his feet and stayed put so she practically bumped into him. The man was going to cause her to pass out if he kept surprising her with this kind of behavior. Her pulse rate rocketed out of control as she looked up at him.

He was looking down at her with a quizzical expression. "I think you have been misled. This is the cowboy way but it's also a man's way. And you deserve it."

Breathe, Lynn. Just breathe.

Her head was spinning with the crazy commotion rioting inside of her. Her pulse was out of control, her head dizzy, her stomach sick—the odd combination shouldn't feel so beautifully wonderful but it did. If her boys complained of the same symptoms she'd have said they had the flu but this was not the flu. This was thrilling.

Chance tilted his head and she knew he was about to kiss her. And she hadn't wanted anything as much, ever.

Almost involuntarily her chin lifted and her eyes closed in anticipation…even as somewhere in the back of her mind she was reminding herself that she didn't trust any man with her heart. She didn't.

Tugging her toward him, Chance wrapped his arms around her. But instead of kissing her he placed his lips against her ear. "I'm so glad God kept you safe and brought you here. You deserve all the good things in life. I hope you truly realize that. You never deserved not to be treated like the lady you are."

Sucking in a sharp breath, Lynn breathed in the masculine, earthy scent of Chance's cologne. Unexpected tears welled in her eyes at the sweetness of his words. All she could do was nod against his neck for fear the dam would open and she would cry. And how horrible would that be, to burst into tears!

He stepped back and gave her a cocky grin and a wink, which pulled an even more unexpected laugh of relief from her.

"Are you ready to eat?" Chance drawled, holding out his arm for her.

"That sounds lovely." Butterflies going nuts, emotions running crazy inside of her, Lynn slipped her hand into the crook of Chance's arm. He immediately covered her hand with his and escorted her into the restaurant. She had never felt so special in all her life.

She knew he was simply being kind but still hc was going out of his way to make her feel good about the evening…and she did.

He pulled her chair out for her and helped her take off her coat. He waited while she ordered first, making certain she ordered exactly what she wanted, her favorite, Chicken Alfredo. And this restaurant made the best she'd ever eaten. Of course, with all the attention Chance was paying her it could have been scorched and five days old and she'd have thought it was the best ever.

Chance Turner seemed like the best man ever. He seemed almost too good to be true. Was he as special as he seemed? Children were good judges of character and Gavin and Jack had adored him from the first…but was it real?

She'd tried and tried not to feel drawn to Chance, but tonight she couldn't deny that she was.

The knowledge scared her to death.

Chapter Fifteen

Lynn was frazzled by the time she made it to the church the next morning. As the secretary she was supposed to open the church office for the visiting preacher. She hadn't slept well and the boys were bouncing off the wall the second their eyes opened. Of course they'd been over-the-moon excited since Chance had brought her to pick them up the night before.

Chance—she shouldn't have been surprised when he'd insisted on taking her to pick them up. Telling her he didn't mind and he would rather know that she and the boys were home safe and sound when he went home. Since there was room in his double-cab truck, she agreed. It was another gentlemanly trait that she wasn't used to…. How had she made such bad choices in her life?

Looking back, if she'd been reading a novel and a character she cared about was heading toward making the bad choices she'd made, as a reader she would have thrown the book across the room in frustration. But, she'd not had the good sense to see what she was doing. She'd been too close to the fire and the smoke had blinded her. Or at least that was the kindest way she could describe her choices…. Life was about choices and she'd chosen badly.

She had had the best evening of her life and then the past had surged up and driven it all away with doubts about herself. How had she chosen to marry her ex-husband? It was humiliating to think love could have blinded her to Drew's character.

Her mood didn't get any better when she walked into the church office and played the message on the answering machine….

Chance drove into the church parking lot earlier than he'd planned. He'd had a restless night after dropping Lynn and her boys off. That he couldn't get Lynn off his mind was an understatement.

Lynn Perry amazed him. And she also confused him. He'd have sworn she'd expected him to be a jerk last night. She wasn't used to the cowboy way, as she'd put it when he'd walked around to open her door for her. What was she used to? His temper had flared in that instant and it had been all he could do not to voice his opinion about her ex-husband in a very ungodly way. Instead, God had held him true to his calling and he'd reacted with positive words for her. She did deserve all the good things in life and he was glad God had brought her through that bad time safely.

Kissing her temple hadn't been in the plan. Holding her had happened out of concern and encouragement… but not wanting to let her go had had nothing to do with either. That had strictly been the man in him.

It was that man in him that was heading toward the

church at eight-thirty when Sunday school didn't start until nine-thirty. Lynn would probably be there early because of the program. She might need more help.

"Chance, Chance!" The twins yelled, running toward him the instant they saw him pull into the parking lot. They'd been sitting on the front steps of the church looking slightly miserable…probably had been instructed not to get dirty, which for them was a real trial.

"What's wrong, fellas?"

"We ain't got no preacher for today," Gavin burst out.

Jack nodded vigorously. "He done canceled and left the church high and dry."

Despite the situation, a smile tugged at Chance's lips at the boy's word choice. App's truck was in the parking lot and he was pretty sure Jack was repeating something he'd heard.

Gavin took his arm. "You got to help us, Chance."

"Yes sirree," Jack quipped, planting his hands on Chance's hip and pushing him forward. "You gotta help us."

This was not what he'd been expecting as he'd driven to the church, but then nothing since he'd arrived in Mule Hollow had gone as he'd expected.

"We brung him to ya, Momma," Gavin said excitedly, ten feet before they reached Lynn, who'd come out of the church office to talk to App.

Lynn had her arms crossed and looked a little stressed out. Applegate's bushy brows were crinkled like crawling caterpillars above thoughtful eyes. "Our stand-in fer the day left us high and dry," he grumbled. "Jest called in and said he wasn't comin'."

"App, now, he said he was ill," Lynn said firmly, giving Chance a look that said her patience was ebbing.

"I didn't miss a day of work in fifty years. You set yor mind to it and you feel better after ya fulfill yor commitments."

"In *fifty* years!" Jack exclaimed. "What's fifty years?"

"It's a bunch, son." App scowled deeper as he hit Chance with a glare. "So I guess it's up ta you, son."

All eyes turned to him. The one thing he was thankful for was that they were the only ones at the church. He didn't expect that to be the case for too much longer though. "App, not so fast. What about Brady?"

Lynn's mouth fell open. "Seriously. You seriously just said that?"

"He did a great job—"

"There was a wreck at the county line that he is dealing with this morning," she said, curtly. "May I speak with you in the office?" She didn't wait for his answer, just took his arm and pulled him along with her. Gavin and Jack fell into step with them. She looked around him. "You boys go play."

"But you said we was in trouble if we got dirt on us," Jack groaned.

"Yeah, that's what you said," Gavin assured her.

Chance would have laughed at the entire situation had it not been hemming him into a corner.

"Boys. Go play, have a good time but please try to stay clean. Can you do that?"

They looked at each other then at their momma. It was clear they weren't really sure if they could do it or not.

"Sure we can," Gavin said, giving his best shot to being positive. Jack didn't look near as sure. "Tell her, Jack."

"What if we get a teensy-bitty little dirt on us?" he asked with a face that made Chance almost bust with laughter.

"Fine. Go play," Lynn said and he knew he was in trouble if she was so zeroed in on talking to him that she'd give them the go-ahead to get dirty before the program.

Still holding on to his arm she marched him to the office and kicked the door shut with her heel. Startled, he half expected her to tell him to sit, as if he was in the principal's office. As soon as the door slammed shut she let go of him and looked up at him like a puppy that had lost its favorite toy. "You have to preach today."

"No. I don't."

The puppy disappeared in a blink. "Chance Turner. What are you doing? You were thanking God for what he did for me and my boys last night but today you still won't go back to preaching. I don't understand."

She was right and he knew it. He hung his head and studied his boots before looking back at her. "You're right. I don't know what I was thinking."

Her expression softened. "Chance, you lost someone you cared about as a person but, more importantly, as a soul you desperately wanted to see in Heaven one day. It affected you. It hurt. Even as the man of God that you are, it affected you. There is nothing wrong with that. It is actually a wonderful thing. I love it—I mean—well, yeah, I love that about you."

He swallowed hard and his heart was thrumming in

his chest at her words. It was true he cared deeply but he'd never before felt like he'd failed on such a personal level. "I can't shake the feeling that I didn't do enough. I needed one more moment with him."

"But who can gauge how many moments a person gets to hear about the Lord before their time is up? No one can. That's not your call. I don't know how to help you. But I have faith that God is in control and He knows your heart, Chance. He knows you wanted more opportunities to be a witness and that you regret not making more. But it's not all about you. It's about Randy. You couldn't make Randy's choices for him or any of your cowboys. You can only present them with God's enduring love for them—you know this."

"I know it. But it's like I'm lost in the yaupon thicket."

Lynn chuckled. "I'm so sorry, but I don't believe I've ever heard it put that way before. But you know that God can get you out of anything. Remember that God is light. If you walk with Him, He will lead you."

"And I thought I was the preacher." Looking at her his spirits lifted. He knew it all, had given advice, scripture and counsel to many, and yet he needed these words and comfort from Lynn. "Thank you."

"So do you think you could bring a few words to the congregation as a prelude to the program? It doesn't need to be a full sermon even. Just whatever God leads you to say. What's it going to be?"

She was so proud of Chance. She sat with the kids on the front row as he stepped to the pulpit. She'd come to realize how much he cared for the bull riders though, and he seemed out of place to her. He was a rodeo preacher, she saw that so clearly now.

He was better suited to his ministry. Or maybe it was simply that she knew his heart through his concern for Randy. But either way she knew the men he led in worship each week were blessed to have a man so heavy with concern for them. She hadn't seen him in action but she knew in her heart of hearts that he was as much a man of faith as any she'd ever been around.

"Good mornin'," he said, his Texas drawl reverberating across the room. "I've been straining against getting in this pulpit since I came home, but God pretty much laid the pathway clean this morning and roped me into it."

Laughter crackled across the sanctuary. Lynn smiled and caught Gavin and Jack completely enthralled watching him. Their little faces were upturned and their eyes bright and unblinking as they grinned at him. "Have you ever heard the saying, don't sweat the petty stuff, and don't pet the sweaty stuff?" He hiked a brow as the laughter rolled, then he sobered. "I told y'all I was a cowboy preacher. But seriously, what I've been dealing with since coming home isn't petty or sweaty, but it's been heavy on my heart. A very wise woman told me that God's got things under control for those who believe in Him." He winked at her from the pulpit and her stomach dropped to her toes.

She listened as he gave a short sermon on 1 John 5-7, *God is light and in Him is no darkness at all*. It was a good reminder that God sent His Son to walk beside all of his children as the light of their path. She loved the way he delivered the message and knew there were many, herself included, who needed the reminder. He had a plainspoken way with words, of cutting to the heart of the matter and she knew that was exactly the kind of preaching cowboys would respond to. There were no flowery embellishments with Chance. He was a straight shooter for the Lord. She understood that was exactly why he wouldn't preach until he felt his own heart was right, or at least on the path to right.

"I'm going to get out of the way now and let these kids get up here and bless y'all with their Christmas pageant. But I want to encourage you that if you haven't saddled up with Christ—if you haven't accepted this very special gift—that you'll do it today, you won't regret it. And if you're like I've been, caught up in the yaupon thicket, tangled up in your problems, then I pray that God will be your light and open your eyes and He will lead you to clear pastures."

The man was a preacher. Not conventional, but he'd touched her heart.

She leaned forward and motioned for the children to take their places as Chance headed toward them. Gavin started to go to his spot then came back to her. "Momma," he whispered loudly. "Why is God gonna put us in a clean pasture?"

Chapter Sixteen

"Those little darlings did so wonderful yesterday!" Esther Mae said as she burst into the candy store with Norma Sue and Adela on her trail. The sleigh bells on the door jingled merrily.

"It was even cuter when Joshua—or should I say the baby sheep—wandered up on the stage and started waving at his momma and daddy and then told them his costume was itching him."

Adela's eyes twinkled. "I thought my Sam was going to fall out of his seat when Joshua started to try and take it off and Gavin and Jack—sweet darlings—tried to talk him out of it. They were really taking on the responsibility of being the older boys of that group."

Lynn could have been embarrassed that the play had ended up being more humorous entertainment than anything but she wasn't. That was part of the joy of getting small children involved in a program. You never knew what was going to happen. She'd loved it. "I hated to have to go up on stage and stop them but Joshua wanted that costume off and I was afraid my two boys were going to wrestle him to try and keep it on him."

She'd tried to get their attention and get them all back into the lineup but they weren't listening. She'd finally looked at Chance, who was about to burst with held-in laughter—not helping her at all. She'd given him a teasing scowl, then walked up the two steps to where the boys were trying to manhandle three-year-old Joshua into keeping on the sheep costume. It was a towel they'd sewn pillow filler on so that it looked fluffy like a sheep. Fuzz was flying everywhere!

"I still haven't figured out what part of that outfit was causing him to itch. The towel was all that touched his neck."

Stacy had been placing a tray of chocolate-covered nuts in the glass display case. She straightened, looking fresh. "I'm just glad Bryce didn't try and strip down to his training pants and join them."

"Lynn stepped in just before everything hit the fan." Norma Sue chuckled. "Anyway, we came by for a couple of things. First, we've got a lot to do this week if we are going to have a wedding Saturday. I'm so glad Chance agreed to do this. I think our boy is coming around. He did wonderful yesterday."

"He sure did," Esther Mae gushed. "Hank laughed all the way home. He said he wasn't going to sweat the petty stuff anymore or pet the sweaty stuff. Out of all that was said, *that* is what my Hank got the most out of."

"He said he would preach next Sunday, too." Adela was watching Lynn, who wondered if she was picking up on her reluctance to talk about this. Adela was extremely perceptive. And Lynn had a major problem. As of yesterday she didn't believe that Chance would ever belong in a traditional church setting. Although Mule Hollow was packed to the gills with cowboys and the entire town pretty much lived the cowboy way, it was still hard to think about him sitting in that office day in, day out.

A wide grin cracked across Norma Sue's face as she stared at Lynn. "We've decided to have a Christmas Ball the week before Christmas. So that means we've got a wedding to get ready for, a Christmas Ball and then Christmas. What do y'all think about that?"

"Norma Sue, that sounds like fun," Nive said, coming out of the back. "Doesn't it, Lynn?"

Nive had been giving her a hard time all morning. "It sounds busy."

"Well, sure it is. But we need to do everything we can to encourage Chance while he's here and keep him from staying out there on the property. Him agreeing to do our Stacy's wedding is a good sign. That boy has a heart as big as Texas and he needs to share that with a family. Don't you agree?"

Lynn agreed to come out and help decorate for the wedding and she reluctantly agreed to attend the Christmas Ball, which had matchmaking written all over it! But she kept her mouth shut when it came to agreeing that Chance needed to be the new preacher at the Mule Hollow Church of Faith, or that he needed to share his big ol' heart with a family…namely her family. Maybe he was supposed to have a family but she—well, she might be tempted, but in the end she knew nothing would come of throwing the two of them together.

She wasn't interested in a husband. She guessed she was still tangled up in the yaupon thicket with her eyes tightly shut, because she wasn't seeing any light leading her to a clear pasture. Where being ready for a husband was concerned she wasn't seeing clear pastures anywhere!

No matter how wonderful Chance Turner was.

"I'm tellin' ya it ain't country music," App grunted. He slapped a red checker one spot forward and glanced at Chance and Wyatt as they walked into the diner. "Mornin'," App and Stanley said in unison.

Chance and Wyatt echoed their greetings and took stools at the counter. Growing up, Chance and his cousins used to have races to see who could spin the cowhide-covered stools the fastest. Today he folded his hands on the counter and glanced toward the checker game.

Stanley grinned and made a double-jump move. "Yor right about it," he continued as if his conversation hadn't been paused momentarily to greet the morning stragglers. "No complaints from me. I bet Alan Jackson and George Strait—and I know good and doggone well George Jones—are all wonderin' what's happenin' ta country."

"*Rap* country," App grumbled, so caught up in the discussion that losing two checker pieces didn't even bother him. "Whoever heard of such a thing? It was on every station when I drove into town this mornin'. Three different songs. How many of 'em are out thar?"

Stanley shook his balding head. "It ain't right. Before ya know it they'll be tradin' in thar belts and wearin' thar britches down around thar ankles."

"So how do y'all really feel about it?" Chance teased.

He was feeling better about life in general today. God had helped him start finding his way. And he'd done it through a class act with dark hair and elusive eyes.

"We like yor preachin' a lot more than we like that garbage."

Wyatt cleared his throat. "Well, that's not saying a whole lot by the sound of it. I might be insulted if I was you, cousin."

Chance chuckled. "I'm a rodeo preacher, don't apologize."

The conversation ensued about cowboy preaching and traditional preaching and the differences. He wasn't at all surprised that questions about him and Lynn were interspersed throughout the conversation. He'd not been able to get her off his mind.

He and Wyatt were heading to Pete's Feed and Seed when he saw her leaving the candy store.

"I'll catch up to you in a few," he told Wyatt, drawing a knowing grin. He ignored it and strode across the street toward her. "Hey, Lynn," he called, and as she looked his way he thought he saw a flash of excitement. The idea of her being excited to see him pleased him more than he could explain.

"How are you this morning?" she asked, digging inside her purse.

"I'm good. Hey, I was wondering if you'd like to go to dinner again. I thought we could take the boys out. You know, reward them for a good job yesterday."

She stopped digging. "That's funny, Chance."

"Hey, they were only trying to help out and you have to remember they were shepherds watching out for their flock. They just went and tried to gather up their stray."

She laughed, making him smile at the bubbly sound of it.

"I keep thinking about that. It was just so cute. But it really was not the program I had envisioned."

"But you know what," he offered, realizing as he spoke that he'd moved mere inches from her. "God was smiling, I'm sure. Little children please Him just like they please us."

"I know." She pulled her keys from her bag. "I need to go pick them up now."

"Hey," he said, not wanting to let her go. "So how about that dinner and a movie?"

She looked like she was going to say no, then she hesitated—and his heart started pounding unevenly with hope. He wanted to spend time with Lynn. He wanted to see that shadow of wariness, of uncertainty, disappear from her eyes. He wanted her to trust him...but was that all?

"The boys, too?"

"Yeah." He grinned, feeling great. "Let's load 'em up and go find an early movie, then grab some pizza."

"You're sure?"

He wanted to run his fingertips across her jaw in a gentle caress. "Absolutely."

She smiled sweetly and her eyes lit up like candles on a birthday cake. "You are so good to my boys. That means so much to me."

His throat had seized up on him at that look. It dug in deep and snuggled into nooks and crannies of his heart. He grinned—it was all he could do for a couple of seconds. He'd almost tried to tell her that she meant so much to him….

"Three."

"Three?"

"I'll pick you up at three. Unless that's too early," he said, as shaken as if he'd just been dragged from beneath the hooves of the biggest, baddest bull of all time.

"That sounds great." She opened her car door. "If you're sure."

Oh, he wasn't sure about anything in that moment except that he had just stepped over a line into a world he had never been in before. "I love your boys, sure I'm sure. It'll be fun."

She was having enough trouble keeping her head out of the yaupon thicket without accepting another date with him! But he'd offered to take her boys. How could she refuse that? And there was absolutely no denying that his offer thrilled her. *He loved her boys.* Those words had melted her.

It was scary. And for a gal who thought she'd gotten her act together, who thought she was seeing life in clear terms—she wasn't. And if God was out there trying to light the way to a clear path she wasn't seeing the light!

Her heart was getting involved in a big way. And with her heart and her emotions involved…she was trying to fight against making any emotional decision where a man was concerned, ever again.

But, a few hours later, it was hard to think straight when the man was buying popcorn for her boys!

Gavin and Jack were jumping up and down with

excitement over the animated movie they were about to see. The fact that they were seeing it with their hero skyrocketed the experience to the moon and back.

"Here you go," Chance said, turning to hand her a tub of popcorn. "If you'll carry this, I'll carry the drinks."

She barely heard him over the blood rushing through her veins at lightning speed. "Got it," she squeaked, when his fingers brushed hers in the handoff. Her stomach was in knots—a combination of thrill and disaster mixed together.

"You boys ready for this?" he asked, handing each one a small drink and leading the way toward the theater.

"I am," Gavin said, carrying his drink very carefully. Lynn knew he was trying to impress Chance by not spilling anything.

"Me, too." Jack practically sang he was so excited. "I want to see that dog fly!"

Chance chuckled. "I think he does a good job of it, from what I heard."

They reached the designated theater along the long hallway and Chance held the door as they entered. As she passed by he leaned close. "Are you having fun?" he asked. His warm breath sent tingles down her neck and racing along her spine.

She turned, startled, and found herself so close that they were practically kissing. "Yes," she said breathlessly. She was embarrassed. His eyes were twinkling.

"Me, too."

His gaze dropped to her lips and for a mere second she thought—

"Y'all comin' or ya just gonna stand there?" Gavin called from the front of the theater.

Thankfully a wall hid them from the people in the seats. She bolted and strode to her boys with Chance right behind her.

It was a great movie. Then again she only came to that conclusion from the boys' delighted reactions to it. They oohed and ahhed all through it. She'd had the storm of the century battling away inside her and the sinking feeling that her boat was about to capsize!

Chapter Seventeen

On Saturday before the wedding Chance was in the church office when Emmett poked his head in the door.

"Chance, got a minute?"

"Sure, I'm at your beck and call today. What's up?"

The cowboy pulled the door shut behind him and stood there with his black hat in his hands. They were both wearing black western-cut jackets and white shirts. Chance kept running his finger around the stiff neck of his shirt, straining against the pull of the western tie. As they looked at each other they grinned, realizing they were both doing the same thing.

"I'm not much for ties and top buttons," Emmett said, taking his hat between both hands.

"Me either. On the rodeo circuit a tie isn't required as preaching attire."

Emmett nodded, as his thoughts went serious. "I need you to pray with me."

On the circuit Chance was used to the tough cowboy who was hard to get to know and even harder to bring to the Lord. He was also used to the cowboy who'd given his life to the Lord and showed up rain or sleet to worship in the arena on Sunday morning before his ride that afternoon. When something was on their hearts it was written across them like the red letters of his Bible. Emmett had something on his heart…Chance had no doubt it was a timid, pale blonde with eyes only for him.

"I'm ready. What's on your mind?"

"I need prayers that I can be the man that Stacy needs. The one who can show her all God's love for her through my love for her."

Chance nodded, understanding full well his concern for his bride-to-be. "That is God's command to all husbands. I've been watching you and I've heard stories about how you've been there for the last two years, demonstrating your love to Stacy in quiet, faithful action. I'm going to pray for you, Emmett, but clearly, God intended your paths to cross and your lives to intertwine. Keep your eyes on God, your priorities in order—God first, your wife second, your children third and everything else after that."

Chance and Emmett knelt beside the desk there in the church office. He placed his hand on Emmett's shoulder, much like he'd done to many a cowboy before, watching him ease over the bars and sink onto the back of his bull. He wasn't standing at the gate but he realized as he prayed that he was in a sense doing that with Emmett and Stacy. This was why she was so intent on the pastor being someone she felt connected to. When they were through with the prayer he gave Emmett a hard handshake and a hug. "You ready?"

Emmett took a deep breath and met Chance with steady, sure eyes. "God said in Genesis that it wasn't good for man to be alone, so he created woman. I've waited my whole life for Stacy. I'm ready."

"I'm proud for you and proud to know you." Chance held out his hand and shook Emmett's. This was a man who walked humbly with God. Chance liked him. "If you're ready, and obviously you are, there's only one thing to say—*Let's ride.*"

"I now pronounce you husband and wife. Emmett, you may kiss your bride."

Lynn dabbed at her tear-stained face as the shy cowboy smiled, then took Stacy in his arms.

Stacy had wanted the three women who came on the bus together from L.A. to No Place Like Home to stand up beside her, Lynn, Nive, Rose. And also Dottie, who'd taught them and inspired them through her ministry at the shelter with Brady. Brady walked down the aisle and it was a touching scene as he handed her over to Emmett. Lynn's heart had ached watching them. Stacy, with so much reason not to trust again, had found love. She'd pushed through all her ugly to love and trust Emmett.

If only she could do that, Lynn would be able to give her sons everything they deserved....

Chance's eyes met hers as Emmett and Stacy kissed and she felt the warmth of his gaze all the way to her toes.

This was a man whose heart was big and bold and concerned with the things of the Lord. A man whose heart had broken because he felt he'd failed God and Randy. This was a man who loved God. A man who enjoyed spending time with her boys and whom her boys clearly loved. They talked about him nonstop, even more since the movie and pizza night. What a man he was.

Yes, Lynn. This is the man you can trust.

The words jumped out at her...as did the knowledge that Chance was a man she could love.

Chance didn't get to talk to Lynn at the reception. She seemed to always be where he wasn't. And she always seemed to be busy. Since Stacy had opted to have her reception at the small fellowship hall at the church rather than the community center, he felt pretty confident that Lynn was avoiding him. The place was only about as big as a doctor's waiting room. Lynn was keeping out of his way, no doubt about it.

After the birdseed was thrown and the happy groom tucked his wife safely into the seat belt of his truck, Chance stood on the sidewalk and talked with different people who came by to visit. Several women asked if he would consider doing their weddings when the time came. It had been a hard question to answer but he told them to call him.

"You might have started something," Cole said, coming up to stand beside him. They were on the church lawn and dusk was settling in. Through the window he could see Lynn and the other ladies cleaning up. Children were running around playing inside and also on the playground. He couldn't see them since they were out front, but he could hear the familiar whooping and hollering of Gavin and Jack. Those two boys were full of life.

It was a great evening. Though he was troubled by

thoughts of Lynn, Chance felt a sense of peace and contentment. "Lots of gals have marriage on their minds."

Cole chuckled. "That's why they come here. Can you believe how alive this place has gotten?"

"It's always been a great place but it is nice seeing babies and families again." He remembered how it had been coming home to the weathered town. Mostly working cowboys and the town itself just a tired-looking bunch of buildings slowly going downhill.

"Uh-oh, here comes trouble." Cole grinned as Applegate, Stanley and Sam came striding up looking like stair steps. Sam, the shortest of the bunch, held out his hand.

"That was great," the wiry man said, shaking in his normal iron grip. "Ya did a fine thang, marrin' those two off."

"Yup," App boomed, clamping down on Chance's hand as soon as Sam let go.

Chance shook Stanley's hand, then crossed his arms over his chest. "I'm glad I did it. They're a special couple."

"That's the pure truth." Stanley eyed his buddies. "We've come on official business, Chance."

Cole tucked his fingers in his pockets, giving him an are-you-ready-for-this look. In the back of Chance's mind he'd known this was coming. He'd known the moment he'd stepped into that pulpit a week ago. He just hadn't expected official business to happen right after Stacy and Emmett's wedding.

App cleared his throat and pushed back his thin-as-a-beanpole shoulders. He started to speak, then paused...

maybe for effect but it was time enough for Chance to intervene and stop them. He didn't though. A month ago, before Randy's death, he wouldn't have let them get started. Today, he kept his mouth shut.

"We are officially offering you the position as our preacher."

Cole was watching him, no twinkle in his usually laughing eyes. Chance was honestly confused. Why hadn't he just told them no?

The annex door suddenly flew open and Norma Sue came barreling out with her hands in the air. "Move out of the way, boys, a baby's comin' through!"

Behind her Clint Matlock was supporting Lacy as she walked. And behind them was everyone else. Lacy was grinning and grimacing simultaneously as she moved the way only pregnant women could do. Her hand was on her rounded belly and she leaned back into the support of Clint's arm.

Clint looked about as shaken as Chance had ever seen him. Then again, it was that I'm-about-to-be-a-daddy look. It was chock-full of the realization of the responsibility that was about to hit his shoulders.

Chance wasn't about to be a daddy but he knew that feeling. As a preacher he felt it for his cowboy congregation all the time. He'd walked away for a little while but he still felt it.

"I should have known the baby was going to take after his momma," Clint said as he passed them. "She's always full of surprises."

"And you know you love it—ow!" Lacy's laugh cut to a grunt.

"Y'all better stop talking and hoof it on to this here

car," Norma Sue bellowed from the middle of the parking lot.

Esther Mae wore a huge red hat with a Christmas flower on it. She whipped it off, exposing her flaming-red hair, and began fanning Lacy as she trotted along beside her. "You just hold your horses, Norma Sue. We will get there when we get there. Lacy doesn't need to have this baby on the church parking lot!"

There was a flurry of advice as everyone spread out in an arch, as if the wave of their energy would get Clint and Lacy to the car sooner.

"Here, I'm going to carry you," Clint said, and gently swept Lacy into his arms.

"But walking is better!"

"Lacy—I'm carrying you," Clint growled.

The petite blonde didn't give him any other protest.

"Lacy," Sheri, her best friend snapped as she hurried to keep up with Clint. "Do not have that baby in the car. Do you understand? You love that ol' thing but this baby does not need to come into this world in the backseat of an Elvis throwback!"

Lacy chuckled. "I'll do my best."

Chance had fallen into step with Lynn as she passed by him. She looked up at him with dancing eyes.

"This is so exciting," she said. "Lacy's having a baby!"

They reached Lacy's 1958 pink Caddy. Norma Sue was holding open the door and Clint eased Lacy into the seat.

Grinning, he jogged around and doubled up as he crawled behind the wheel. "I'll see y'all in a minute."

"We'll be hot on your trail," Sam said, putting his arm around Adela's shoulders.

"We are praying." Adela patted Clint's shoulder before he pulled the door shut and gassed it.

In a flurry of movement, everyone headed toward their vehicles.

"Are they safe in that crazy car?" Chance asked, still watching the pink monstrosity of a car's big fin taillights disappear into the dusky evening.

Lynn chuckled. "That car's in great shape. Lacy brings it to all the weddings because she likes the nostalgia of it. Clint enjoys his wife's quirks so he goes along with it. I think he'd have rather had the truck on this occasion though. He looked so nervous."

Chance agreed. "It's understandable."

"They goin' to the hospital to pick up their baby?" Gavin asked as he and Jack came running up from the back of the church.

"They sure are," Lynn said.

"This place is growin'!" Jack exclaimed, then paused. "We need to go to the hospital and pick us up a baby. They're funny."

Chance laughed at the alarmed look on Lynn's beautiful face. "Would y'all like to go to the hospital and wait for the baby to be born?"

"You mean we got to wait on it?" Gavin looked perplexed.

"I'm afraid so." Lynn smiled at Chance and his heart almost tripped over itself with the thrill of it.

"Lynn," Dottie called from the group where she was chatting. "If you want to go to the hospital I'll take the boys home with me. We're keeping Bryce for

Stacy—Brady and I can't go anyway. Nive is going to stay and help me."

"I'll drive you," Chance offered.

"No, I can—"

"That would be great," Dottie said, interrupting Lynn before she could say no. "Lynn, you go now. With Chance. There is no sense you driving there yourself when he's offering."

"But," she started, then looked resigned to the idea. "You're right. Thanks for the offer, Chance."

If he hadn't figured out before that she was avoiding him he would have figured it out now. They said goodbye to the boys and had to repeat to them that only Lacy would be bringing home a baby.

Chance planned on finding out why Lynn didn't want to be around him. He was glad she was riding with him—even if it had taken Dottie's intervention. And not just because he wanted to spend time with her. He needed advice, a sounding board, and though he had three cousins whom he valued considerably…it was Lynn, despite her reluctance to be here with him, whose advice he wanted.

Lacy Brown Matlock gave birth to a nine-pound three-ounce baby boy twenty minutes after Clint fishtailed into the Ranger hospital emergency entrance. Leave it to Lacy to ignore the ultrasound's prediction!

The waiting room was full. The nurses and doctors had grown accustomed to Mule Hollow showing up in force for the birth of their babies.

Lynn smiled through the glass. "He's beautiful."

"I don't see how you can tell with his face all

scrunched up like that," Chance teased. He was standing beside her. The drive to the hospital had been strained. They'd talked about the wedding and the baby and also about the boys wanting her to bring home a baby. She'd chuckled about that but changed the subject quickly when she started wondering if Chance wanted children.

"He looks just like Clint," Norma Sue said. "He won't like being called beautiful."

"But he is," Esther Mae cooed. Her face almost touched the glass as she peered at baby Matlock.

Lynn was so happy for Clint and Lacy but her mind kept going to Chance. *He's the man you can trust.*

The words wouldn't leave her.

"You sure are quiet," Chance said when they finally headed toward the truck.

It was nine o'clock and a northern wind was whipping the pink skirt of her bridesmaid dress around her knees as Lynn walked toward the truck. "I'm sorry. I just have a lot on my mind."

"There's a drive-in up the road. Do you want to stop and get a soda? I'm a good listener and I need to talk to you about something, too."

He opened her door for her and took her elbow as she stepped up and sat in the high seat. Her pulse was racing as she found herself eye-to-eye with him. "That sounds great," she managed. They were in the middle of the hospital parking lot sitting directly beneath a safety light but it didn't matter. She lifted her hand and touched his jaw. His eyes flared in surprise at her touch. "You did an awesome thing today, marrying Stacy and Emmett. Thank you."

"I'm glad I did. It meant a lot to me, too." He placed his hand over hers, pulled it away from his jaw and kissed the back of her hand. "Thank you for pressing me to do it."

The touch of his lips very nearly brought tears to her eyes. The gesture was so sweet. She nodded—it was all she could do. Thankfully he took a breath, backed up and closed the door with a smile. *Get hold of yourself, woman!* She watched as he hurried around the truck. By the time he climbed in, at least she was no longer thinking about throwing herself into his arms.

Chapter Eighteen

Chance pulled into a drive-in spot and, after they'd decided what they wanted to drink, he pushed the button on the microphone. "When I'm on the road I eat at more of these places than I want to think about. It's not something about my work that I enjoy."

Lynn tilted her head to the side. "We didn't have to stop."

He cocked a brow. "I didn't say I wasn't enjoying it right now."

She smiled, despite the thoughts in her head. The thoughts of how she enjoyed being with him. Of how she knew in her heart that she could trust him. And the thought that had her insides so tied up that she'd almost not been able to concentrate on the amazing new baby that had just come into the world…. She was falling in love with Chance.

Falling might not be the right word but it was the only one she was willing to acknowledge. *Fallen* was too—she just couldn't accept that it had actually happened. The idea put her in shock. Falling in love was still controllable. She could stop it.

How was this all clashing around inside her while she was sitting calmly at the drive-in with Chance with fifties music playing in the background?

"Do you want to talk about why you're so quiet and why you were avoiding me after the ceremony?"

"No."

"You sure gave that a lot of thought." The girl brought their drinks and he was distracted momentarily while he paid her.

Lynn took the moment to talk herself off the ledge. No, she wasn't going to tell the man that she was quiet because she'd realized she'd fallen in love when he'd pronounced Stacy and Emmett man and wife…. *Fallen*— she'd just admitted it to herself. She closed her eyes and tried to breathe. Tried to backtrack and replace *fallen* with *falling*.

But it was hopeless. She knew that she'd used the right word. She had fallen for him but it was hopeless nonetheless. It didn't change anything…. It didn't.

He handed her the drink and watched as she took a long sip through the straw. "You said you had something you needed to talk to me about," she said, hoping to take the focus away from her.

His gaze narrowed, telling her she wasn't fooling him. He set his drink in the cup holder without taking a drink. "I've been officially asked to be the preacher at the church."

"You told them no, didn't you."

His brows dipped. "You didn't hesitate on that."

"No. I didn't. You did a great job but, unlike everyone else trying to put you in the pulpit, I believe you already have yours."

"So I guess you're still holding it against me that I talked about sweat in my sermon."

She wasn't finding much funny right now so didn't laugh. "I never held that against you. I just think your heart is in the arena with your riders. You don't need to give that up because you lost one."

Chance looked troubled. She realized then that he'd been troubled all along—it had just been hidden beneath a thin surface. "What if I have other reasons for wanting to stick around Mule Hollow?"

"My Girl" was playing in the background as he set steady green eyes on her. A shiver of awareness coursed over her and she could barely breathe with the knowledge of what he was thinking…. Surely she was wrong.

"You love the rodeo circuit and preaching. They need you." She set her drink in the holder. "And my boys need me. We'd better get back."

She pulled her eyes away from him but could feel his gaze on her as she put her seat belt back on. The inside of the truck was closing in quickly. She willed her emotions to calm and her good sense to rule. She was not looking for love. She was not looking for a wedding.

She and her boys were fine.

Chance drove. He pressed his boot to the gas pedal and glued his eyes on the road ahead of him. He'd almost told Lynn he wanted to stick around Mule Hollow because of her. And her boys. He'd almost told her that… he loved her. At the drive-in soda stop, no less.

The look in her eyes and her reaction told him she wasn't ready to hear him. He hadn't known until standing beside her looking at the baby that he was ready to say anything. The truth had come calmly over him, with a sense so sure and strong that it reminded him of the day he'd committed his life to the Lord. There had been no turmoil in that moment. It was as if God had been standing beside him that day and simply asked him, "Do you love me?" Chance had known the answer was yes right then. Before that moment, he'd been fighting a battle over living for God or being caught up in the world. But on that day he'd known he was forever changed. Standing beside Lynn he'd known that same peace and clarity. He loved her. He wasn't certain what the next step was, but that didn't change the fact that he loved her.

He loved Lynn Perry. It was a beautiful thing.

"Are you all right?" he asked after they'd ridden fifteen miles in silence. He wanted to pull the truck over and tell her how he felt but he knew now wasn't the time. He was worried about her.

"I'm fine. But Chance, you shouldn't make a decision like this suddenly. You told me how much it means to you to be there for those cowboys on the road. I'd hate to see you make a mistake."

"Why don't you think I could be happy at the church?"

"I guess I don't know that."

"How do you feel about us?" The question came out before he could stop it. He glanced at her. She looked stressed at his question. Her hands were clasped in her lap and her lips were pressed tightly together as she stared straight ahead.

She didn't answer for at least a mile. He couldn't say anything. He was tied up like a ball of yarn inside.

"Chance, I didn't—"

"Hold on," he said, knowing he had to stop her. He pressed the brake and moved the truck to a shuddering stop on the edge of the road. They were within fifteen miles of Dottie and Brady's house and there was no way he wasn't finishing this conversation. Or letting her answer too quickly.

He put the truck in park, opened his door and got out. He could feel her watching him as he stomped around the front of the truck. He opened her door, reached around her and unsnapped her seat belt.

"Chance, what are you doing?"

He stared straight into her eyes, took her hands and tugged her out of the truck. He gently cupped her face in his hands and held her still as he searched her eyes for any sign of the same feelings that were raging through him. He lowered his head and, when she didn't protest, he touched his lips to hers.

His heart was lost for certain in that moment. There was no turning back for him. He thought back to his prayers with Emmett and had a new understanding. He knew that he would wait for Lynn Perry's heart to heal and pray for her to love and trust him for as long as it took. To his surprise she melted against him and returned his kiss in a sweet, hesitant response. Hope filled him. She wasn't averse to him. She hadn't slapped him or pushed him away. She'd kissed him.

Joy filled his soul.

"You snuck up on me, Lynn," he said, moving his hands to her shoulders as he held her close and spoke against her ear. "I came home to be alone and to search my heart for answers from God and, instead of letting me be alone, God put you in my pathway. I love you, Lynn. I've been falling for you from the first moment we met."

Her hands dug into his back at his words and she stiffened in his arms. He could feel her heart pounding and could sense the strain that his words put on her. Was it fear? Was it that she couldn't trust him? Either way, it stung. "I'm not your ex-husband, honey. You don't have anything to fear from me. I would never hurt you or your boys. You can trust me."

She took a deep breath. "I don't know how to deal with this, Chance. I just don't know."

Her words were so full of angst that a helpless feeling washed over him and he asked God to intervene. "You can pray and we can take this one step and one day at a time."

She pushed back from him. "I care for you, Chance. There is no denying that. I love the way you are with my boys. I love the heart that you have for others and their relationship to the Lord. You are a wonderful man and I am so blessed these last few weeks knowing you and all the help you've given me."

The man in him wanted her to return his love instantly. But he knew she had issues from her past that were holding her back. She'd been honest from the beginning that she had a problem with trust. He'd been forewarned. "Then there is hope for me."

"I can't promise you anything. I'm afraid you'll be hurt—"

"The only way I'm going to be hurt is if you tell me right now that there is no hope for us."

Her eyes were bright and her lips trembled. "I want there to be hope."

Joy as bright as sunlight split a shaft straight through him. "You can't even imagine how happy that makes me." He ran his fingertips along her jaw, loving the feel of her. "Let's take it nice and easy, one day at a time." When she nodded, he closed his eyes and thanked God. Opening them, he found her watching him. Slowly he touched his lips to hers, relishing the sweet scent of her…. His longing to hear that she loved him intensified. This was what it was all about. Finding someone to share his life with was the best blessing.

"So how's everything going?"

Lynn looked up from working on the church bulletin to see Lacy walk in holding a baby carrier.

"Lacy, you're out and about!" she exclaimed, coming out of her chair to hug Lacy. "I have to see Tate."

Lacy gently pulled the baby blanket away and exposed the infant's face. He was sleeping soundly. "Isn't that the cutest kiddo you've ever seen?"

"He is so cute. I like his name, too. I was surprised when you didn't name him Elvis."

Lacy smiled. "I love his music, and his taste in cars. But I wanted my baby to have his own name. Be his own man. Of course if God could give him a voice like Elvis I wouldn't complain."

Lynn itched to pick him up but didn't ask. She knew he'd be held too much as it was. Instead she sat back down. "What are you doing out?"

"Clint told me to stay home but I just can't. I thought I'd come bring this thank-you card by so you could put it in the bulletin."

"Sure I can." She took the card and opened it to read.

"So I hear you and Chance are an item."

Lynn's head whipped up. "An item?"

"Calm down, don't throw your neck out," Lacy chirped. "I was down at the diner with Clint and little Tater—yeah, App, Stanley and Sam have already nick-named him Tater Man! Boy, did I have that coming."

Lynn laughed. "You walked right into that, didn't you."

"Did I ever. That boy is going to grow up getting called everything from Tater Man to Tater Tot. I thought about naming him Cas but realized he'd get called things like Castor Oil or something. Anyway, I heard Cole and Seth saying Chance had been over at your house almost every day this week. Girlfriend, that makes you an item in our books."

"Oh, well, I cooked and he helped the boys repair my front porch. And, well, he's alone and so he helped us decorate the tree—"

"And in there somewhere did you happen to kiss the cowboy?"

Lynn swallowed hard and met Lacy's twinkling eyes. "Lacy!"

"Hey, come on, Lynn, tell me you are stepping out. Tell me you are taking courage and moving forward with this handsome hunk of man God has put in your path."

"I'm trying."

Lacy sat on the edge of her seat and tapped her plum-colored nails on the desk for a second as her mind whirled behind her electric-blue eyes. "You have been an inspiration to me ever since you stepped off of that bus two years ago. You have fought hard to help yourself, the women who came with you and everyone who has come through those shelter doors. And yet you are afraid. I've been praying you let God set you free."

Lynn stood up and paced to the tiny window. She stared out toward the swings where her boys would normally be playing while she worked on the bulletin. Today they were riding horses with Chance. They were thrilled. She was in deep, and happier than she could ever remember, but she couldn't shake her fear.

"I'm frightened, Lacy."

"Of what?"

"Myself."

Lacy was startled. "I don't understand."

"I don't know how to take the step to the next level. I've reached a comfortable place in my life and, as wonderful as Chance is, I'm terrified I'm going to break his heart."

"Don't break it. Simple as that. Do you love the man?"

Lynn knew she did but there was more to it than that. "I loved Drew, too."

Lacy had stopped drumming her nails on the desk and now she tapped only her index finger methodically like a clock. Lynn could almost see her mind ticking along to the beat.

"You don't trust yourself, that's what you mean?"

Lynn nodded. "I'm comfortable finally. I'm not afraid

as long as I'm not thinking about love and marriage. Every time I look at Chance and think about taking that step I freeze up."

"Then chill and give it time. God is the great healer. I'm sure Chance totally understands this. Has he talked about marriage yet?"

"No. I'm trying to talk him into going back on the rodeo circuit."

"So you're the one keeping him out of this office. Does App know this?" Lacy teased.

"I just want him to be happy and I'm afraid this isn't right for him."

Lacy stood up and plopped a hand on her hip. "I'll pray for you, sister, but why don't you stop worrying about what is right for Chance. He's a big boy, I bet he can figure that out…. You just concentrate on what's right for you, and God's going to take you straight through this to blue skies if you let Him."

Blue skies, clear pastures. Lynn sure wished one of the two would show up. And soon. She'd been having a wonderful and horrible week at the same time. And the worst part was that Gavin and Jack could get hurt if she didn't come to some sort of decision soon about what to do with her life.

"Are you going to the ball tomorrow night?" Lacy asked, lifting the baby carrier.

"Yes, Chance is taking me."

"You go, girl. Go have a good time and stop worrying. God's got this!"

Lynn herded the boys into the car after Lacy left the church and they headed toward the shelter. She'd promised Sandra she'd come by this afternoon. Despite their conversations about what Sandra had done right, she wasn't doing well. Guilt was eating at her. The therapist was working with her, too, but Dottie said she'd withdrawn even more over the last day.

Dear Lord, Lynn prayed as she drove, *give me the words that will help ease Sandra's pain. That will help her understand that she's done the right thing in getting out of the dangerous, abusive situation she was in…for her sake and her child's sake.*

She ended with a prayer for God's will and thought about His place in her own life. Was she allowing God to have His will? Loving and trusting were intertwined in marriage. In her mind there was no way to have one without the other. Only her problem wasn't trusting Chance—how could she not? She didn't trust herself.

When she arrived at the shelter she knew immediately that something wasn't right. Brady's patrol vehicle was parked in front along with Deputy Zane Cantrell's. Dottie was in the yard talking to them.

"Hey, Mr. Brady, hey, Mr. Zane!" the boys called as they raced over and got big hugs from both men. Lynn's heart swelled at the sight.

"What's going on?" she asked as soon as the boys went to play on the swings.

Dottie was pale. "Sandra's gone. She called her husband and told him where she was. He showed up and she and Margaret left with him."

"No," Lynn gasped, looking at Brady and Zane as if believing they would tell her that Dottie was wrong. "But you should have stopped her."

Brady's serious gaze was steady. "She never filed

charges and she left of her own free will. You know our hands are tied."

It was true, but Lynn wanted with all her heart to go after Sandra. To beg her to listen. To beg her to accept that the situation she was in wasn't going to get any better.

But it was too late.

Too late.

Chapter Nineteen

"And may I say you are looking particularly lovely tonight." Chance was on top of the world. He'd spent most of his week working around Lynn's house. He'd arrived early, before she left for the candy store, so the boys were able to sleep in and not be hauled out of bed and carried to the shelter for the day. He'd enjoyed them tagging along with him when they woke. They were fascinated with tools, hammers especially, and the front porch was better for it. They'd helped him replace the wood and were now eyeing the old barn with great interest. He'd also taken them riding at the ranch a couple of times and they'd been thrilled.

To give Lynn some space, he'd worked cattle two days on the ranch but had felt bad that he hadn't been there for the boys.

Lynn had told him over and over again not to feel bad about not being there because she understood he had his own business to take care of. He'd chalked that and a few other things up to her not wanting to impose on him. He considered his time with her and the boys as time well spent. Time well enjoyed. Time to cherish.

He hoped she felt the same. Especially after Sandra had left the shelter. The poor woman's decision to go back with her husband had devastated Lynn and she'd been thinking about it a lot. He had tried to talk to her about it—even explained that Lynn couldn't make Sandra's choices for her...no matter how much she wanted to.

He had niggling worries that Sandra's leaving was affecting Lynn on a deeper level than he could reach.

He hoped to help his case tonight and was glad that the weather was cooperating. The stars were like diamonds sparkling in the huge, dark sky as he'd walked to her door and knocked.

Looking at her, his heart lunged into his throat and shut off his air supply. It was a wonder he was able to tease her with his greeting.

She was smiling at him but in her eyes he saw the same tension that had concerned him all week. Even before Sandra had left, that edge in Lynn's eyes had him worrying that she was putting up a brave front before she broke and ran. It had him on his knees every night asking God to let her trust him.

"Hey, don't look at me like that," he said, determined to keep his voice light. "You do look lovely tonight."

She looked down at the jeans, boots and red sweater she wore. "I'll take your word for it then."

He leaned against the door frame and punched his hat off his forehead then gave her his best Turner smile. "Believe me, my word is good," he drawled nice and slow, even though he wanted to growl in frustration. No matter how good the week had been, her trust issues were hanging in the balance—in that look in the edge of her eyes. Frustrated by his lack of patience he gave up the nonchalant pose and straightened. His nerves were humming tonight. "Where are the boys?"

"Dottie picked them up on her way back from town."

He was disappointed. "We could have taken them."

"It's all right. Dottie didn't mind."

"It wouldn't have been a bother." Nothing about her or her boys was a bother to him. "I enjoy seeing them."

She nodded but instead of saying anything she picked up her purse from the hall table and pulled the door shut. "I guess we better go."

He nodded though the way she'd said the words settled in his gut like lead. Something wasn't right.

The community center was packed by the time they arrived. Lynn had been feeling downhearted all afternoon and felt guilty that she'd basically shot down Chance's good mood. It was mean and selfish and yet she'd done it anyway. She knew it was because of the pressure from the week. She was worried for Sandra and Margaret and heartbroken that Sandra had chosen to go back to her husband. But she above everyone else understood how mixed up Sandra's mind and heart were at the moment. Lynn had thanked God several times since yesterday that He had given her the strength to break free of Drew.

But with every second Chance spent with her boys the pressure built. Could she go back into a relationship again? Could she be totally free from the scars left from her marriage? She had to make a decision and she had to make it now. The potential for her boys' hearts getting broken was escalating and, no matter what Lacy or anyone else said, sitting back and just letting God handle it was not working for her.

She'd done that before—true, the situation had been different. Drew had been violent and manipulative while Chance was wonderful and loving. But if she couldn't give her heart over to trusting and fully loving Chance, she was going to have to pull away before everyone got hurt. With Drew she was the one who had finally made the break. Not God. And this relationship with Chance was on her shoulders, too.

Music was playing in the background. Mule Hollow's cowboys had talent. There were several who could sing like Nashville gold, and as Lynn and Chance entered the building Bob Jacobs was singing a Tim McGraw love song. Love songs…she was in trouble.

The room was decorated with Christmas lights strung about the ceiling. Garlands of colorful lights hung around the doorways. On the small stage they'd set a metal horse trough and filled it with Christmas presents. Beside the trough was a brightly decorated Christmas tree.

"This looks great," Chance said as they entered.

"It does," Lynn murmured, very aware of his hand resting between her shoulder blades. She fought to appear collected.

"Y'all came!" Esther Mae exclaimed from a table near the door. "Come over here and sign your names. We want a record of all who attended. That way next year we can look back and see how many of the couples who came tonight ended up getting married."

She smiled and looked from Chance to Lynn.

Lynn's stomach hurt. Chance gave her a humorous wink that Esther Mae was thrilled to see.

"Y'all make the cutest couple. Babies would be so sweet."

"Hang on, Esther Mae," Chance said, coming to the rescue. "Don't get too far ahead of the plan. I'm just thankful tonight that Lynn came with me at all."

Lynn smiled and touched his arm. "I've got two already," she said to anyone listening. She felt defensive.

"And they're two good ones to have," Chance said, giving her a look that said he understood. "It's good to see you, Esther Mae. We'll get out of your way so the next ones can sign up."

The bouncy redhead waved them off. "Chance, you be sure and dance with Lynn," she called as they were mixing into the crowd.

"I'm planning on doing just that," he said in Lynn's ear as he leaned in and spoke only to her. "You doing okay? You look upset."

The man was too perceptive. "I'm fine, just feeling stressed."

He draped his arm across her shoulders and gently pulled her into the crook of his side. She had the urge to rest her head against his shoulder but she didn't.

"Don't stress, Lynn. Just relax and enjoy the time here with our friends. Don't let Esther Mae upset you. She didn't mean to put too much pressure on you."

That made her laugh. He did, too.

"Okay, so I take that back. She meant it but she didn't mean it to make you feel bad. She meant it out of love and concern for you, and for me, for that matter."

Lynn took a deep breath and momentarily enjoyed being so close to him. There had been times during the week that he'd kissed her when the boys weren't around. And he'd kissed her before he'd left each night. And each time she'd felt like she could kiss him for the rest of her life. She'd felt a longing for more, for the loving relationship, physically and emotionally, that God meant for a married husband and wife to have. She'd missed out on the true relationship that God had intended a marriage to be…. She wanted it.

But there was the risk involved. The heartache. The disillusionment. Depressed, she tried to force the thoughts from her mind.

"Come on, what you need is a little two-step." Chance grinned and swept her out onto the dance floor. "You know, my grandmother called this exercise, not dancing."

Lynn would have laughed but she was trying to concentrate on getting the steps right. She hadn't danced in years. Not since she was in high school. Chance was careful to keep a respectable distance between them as he held her hand in his and kept his arm draped across her shoulders. Cole and Susan danced past them, enjoying the song and time together. Stacy was on the dance floor with Emmett, having returned from their honeymoon at the beginning of the week.

Lynn should have relaxed. She told herself to breathe deep and relax. To enjoy the moment and the prospect of the future she and Chance could have…but Drew's face and all the manipulation that he'd put her though slammed into her with such force that she couldn't even hear the music any longer. Her past was the past, but it clung to her like dirt. She'd hoped loving Chance would wipe it away but it was still there. Thoughts of all she'd been through with Drew sucked the enjoyment out of moments like this.

"Lynn, you're crying," Chance said, looking closely at her. His eyes were so concerned.

"No," she said, but knew it wasn't true as she blinked hard and fought off tears welling in her eyes. She had never been so thankful for low lighting in all her life. "I'm sorry, Chance."

He dipped his head as he slowed their two-step and met her gaze. "Don't be sorry, but I think maybe we need to go outside and talk about this."

She nodded, afraid to speak. Afraid of crying and just as afraid of what she knew she was going to say.

Chance had a bad feeling.

As soon as they'd gone outside Lynn had told him she wanted to go home. He'd said sure, asked if she felt bad, and she'd said she just needed to go home. She'd refused to say anything the entire six miles from town. His heart felt heavy for her. She was fighting demons from her past, he was certain. *Dear Lord,* he prayed, *give me the words to help free her from the wrong that has been done to her.*

The Christmas lights were on, cheerily welcoming them to her home. He half expected the boys to run out of the house and throw themselves at his legs like they loved to do, but they weren't home. He'd started to go get them but she'd said no. She'd simply wanted to go home and after that she'd been silent.

His heart was aching and fear gripped him as he

parked. He started to get out but she placed her hand on his arm and stopped him.

"Chance. Wait. I'm so sorry, but this isn't going to work."

"Lynn. Give it time. I love you and I believe—no, I *know* you love me. I want to marry you and have a future with you. It can be wonderful—"

"It's not that simple, Chance."

She'd been on the verge of tears at the ball but now she was calm. Her voice was steady and her beautiful midnight eyes as clear and bright as a night sky lit by a full moon. It was that calmness that scared him the most.

"I can't, Chance. I just can't do this. You have a life, too, and it's out there on the rodeo circuit. Not here tied down." She opened her door.

"Lynn, don't do this. I'm not going to get out now, because I know you need time to think. But pray about it—"

She nodded and as she closed the door he saw a tear run down her cheek. He couldn't take it. He pushed open the door and was storming around the truck in seconds. He'd let Randy go the wrong direction because he hadn't taken action. He would not do that with Lynn.

She was standing in the headlight beam wiping tears from her eyes when he reached her. He took her by the arms. "I can't force you to do something you don't want to do. Or that you can't do. I can't force you to trust me. I can't take your past away. Or get rid of your emotional or physical scars. I couldn't make Randy's choice for him. You couldn't make Sandra's choice for her. There are some things we are not in control of, but this I know…I can love you. I can and will protect you, from here on out." He pulled her into his embrace but she pulled away.

"I don't want a man to have to protect me. I'm going to protect myself."

"So that's what this is. You are protecting yourself. From me?"

"From anyone."

"From me." He clarified. It was obvious what she meant. "I would never hurt you."

"I know," she said.

"Then what is this?"

She took a deep breath. "This is me protecting myself."

Chance took a step back. "No. This is you taking the easy way out. God never promised we wouldn't have trouble. As a matter of fact, in His word He says, 'In this life you will have trouble.' You are trying too hard to stay safe. You have to trust God at some point." Chance spun and stalked to his truck. She had to come to him of her own choice. He'd just told her she needed to trust the Lord, and he needed to do the same thing.

But as he got into his truck, it took every ounce of his willpower to hold himself back.

As he drove away he knew she was wrong—his life wasn't on the rodeo circuit. It was here with her and her boys and somehow, some way, he was going to prove it to her.

Chapter Twenty

"Momma, where is Chance?" Gavin asked. It was Christmas Eve night and she was tucking them into their beds.

"He was supposed to be here for baby Jesus' birthday," Jack said.

Both boys were tucked in and staring up at her with their wide eyes. They'd been asking about Chance for the last two days. Ever since Dottie had brought them home the morning after the ball they'd been confused.

She'd waited too long to figure out that the best way to protect them was to play it safe. Chance disagreed with her but she couldn't help that. In her mind she'd waited too long and now she knew this breakup was going to hurt them. But it wouldn't hurt as bad as it could have if she'd kept on seeing Chance and things hadn't worked out. No. Despite the fact that it was going to hurt them now she knew it was better this way. Her own heart—well, she couldn't think about that.

The thought of actually crossing the line into giving control of her life over to someone else again scared her to death. Yes, Rose and Stacy had moved on. But everyone dealt with abuse and heartache in different ways. She'd thought she was the strongest of all the women when she'd boarded the bus and headed to Mule Hollow. Well, she wasn't. She couldn't resolve her feelings about the past and she couldn't move forward into a relationship, no matter how desperately she wanted it to work.

But still, she hated to tell Gavin and Jack that Chance wouldn't be coming around anymore. And she couldn't bring herself to tell them now, on the eve of Christmas. But what else could she do? She'd walked right into this.

She sat on the edge of Jack's bed, which was a mere arm's length from Gavin's. "Chance isn't going to be here in the morning," she said gently and saw their expressions fall instantly.

"But why?" Jack asked.

Gavin sat up. "He promised."

Because I can't let him be here.

"But Santa Claus is coming and we're gonna read the story of baby Jesus 'cause that's what Christmas is really about," Jack said solemnly.

She smoothed his hair and kissed the top of his head. Then she moved to Gavin's bed and hugged him. "Come on, lie back down. We'll talk more in the morning but right now you two need to go to sleep."

"He's gonna come," Gavin said. "He said a man's word was his bond."

"Yeah," Jack said, bolting upright. "His integ-itchy means everything. God wants us to grow up to be that."

Lynn's stomach twisted and her heart felt heavier than

it already was, which was hard to believe. "It sounds like you've been having lots of interesting conversations this week."

Both boys' eyes were solemn. "We want Chance to be our daddy, Momma," Gavin said.

"We done asked God for him," Jack said.

Lynn swallowed the lump in her throat, felt the scald of tears fighting for release and the burn in her heart—she wanted this for them, too. She wanted Chance but... she had to make the right choice.

"Let's say our prayers, guys, and then get some sleep. Tomorrow will be a good day." She pushed other thoughts from her head and concentrated on the celebration of Jesus' birth.

Both boys closed their eyes and prayed for Chance to be their daddy.

Lynn hardly slept. She lay down but her heart was heavy and her thoughts were full. She'd missed Chance so much since sending him away. She pulled her Bible into her lap and stared at the verse that jumped out at her. Jeremiah 29:11, "'For I know the plans I have for you,' declares the Lord. 'Plans to prosper you and not to harm you, plans to give you hope and a future.'" It was the life verse of the shelter. It was a verse she grasped with all her heart. But she'd believed she was seeing her future here in this house with her boys. And then Chance entered the picture, and all the pain of her past was stirred up and the clarity she'd thought she'd found was muddied up as thick as riverbed sludge.

She'd prayed for God to give her peace to help her

through this, and she'd yet to find any relief. Sending Chance away had only made it worse.

And now she realized he'd been teaching her boys all week things a man should be. He not only had been teaching them through his actions but also through his words. A man of integrity. That's what he was. And she'd turned him away.

It was five o'clock when something startled her and her Bible slid off her lap beside her. She glanced at the clock and realized that she had dozed off at some point.

"Lynn."

A tapping sound on her window had her bolting straight up, and she was sure she heard Chance calling her name. What?

Scrambling out of bed she hurried to the window. She yanked her housecoat on over her red flannel pajamas and peeked through the curtain. Sure enough, standing in the pale morning darkness was Chance. Tiny sat at his feet looking at him adoringly.

When Chance saw Lynn he smiled. "Can we talk?" he asked.

She nodded, dropped the curtain and almost broke her neck rushing to the back door. *He was here!*

She unlatched the door and hurried out onto the small porch. Chance stood there waiting, strong and steady.

"You came." Her words were breathless.

He nodded, and looked slightly confused by her greeting. "Lynn, I love you. It's been killing me to keep away from you and the boys, but I'm doing it because you asked me to. But I gave them my word, so I have to ask you if I can show up here in a little while."

He'd come. The words kept ringing in her heart and head. *He came. He kept his word to her sons. He was asking her permission. He loved her...he loved them.*

She couldn't speak. So much was in her heart. So much told her this wouldn't work. So much told her it would.

Chance stepped onto the porch but didn't touch her. "Lynn, I can't stand this. You love me." There was a fierceness in his words that dared her to deny it was true. "I've been praying for you. I know trust is hard for you, but can't you please see that I'll never harm you? I want to be your champion. I want to protect you, not to harm you."

God's words echoed in her head. *I have plans for you, Lynn Perry. Plans to prosper you. Not to harm you. Plans to give you, Lynn Perry—you—hope and a future.*

Chance dropped to his knee and took her hand, and her heart stopped beating. "I'm asking you to marry me, Lynn. I'm laying my heart out here so that there is no mistaking what my intentions are. I love you. I love your boys and I love your dog. I love the whole package. I keep thinking I didn't give Randy my everything."

"Oh, Chance."

"I keep thinking I could have done more.... I kept thinking that God should have given me more time. Another chance to get through to him. And then it hit me last night that He did. When Randy asked me to stand at the gate with him, that was my chance. That was a gift from God for me to offer Randy salvation once more. God gave me what I've been grieving about all this time. I just lost it in my confusion. Randy didn't take his last shot at accepting Jesus. I have to rest easy and be at peace with that. But I can't rest easy about us. Not until I give it my all. I am not going to let this be until you know that you mean everything to me. If I could have conveyed to Randy that God loved him even more than I love you, then he'd have seen the splendor of God's love. So I'm putting it all out here. I love you."

His deep voice rasped with emotion. Lynn couldn't breathe.

"Today is the beginning of our hope as a people—this is the morning we celebrate God's Son being born. He loved us so much…. I love you, Lynn. I'll take it slow and patiently."

Lynn was crying. Her heart cracked wide open as he poured his soul out to her. All her defenses were wiped away as she cupped his upturned face, knowing without doubt that with God and Chance beside her she could conquer the fears, the doubts and the leftover hang-ups of her past. Tears blurred her vision as she bent and kissed him. "I love you, Chance. I love you so much."

He kissed her and rose to his feet as he did so, pulling her close.

"*Tiny!*" two small voices squealed from inside the house. Lynn spun and she and Chance hurried inside to see what was wrong. She'd left the door open and Tiny had taken it as an invitation. The horse of a dog was half crouching and looked as if he'd stopped mid-stride, having been found out by Gavin and Jack. He had a big ball of red flannel fuzz she'd cleaned out of the dryer's lint catcher billowing out of his mouth. He was looking up at them all with guilty eyes.

Lynn hurried forward and gently took the lint from his mouth. "Give me that, young man, before you choke on it."

He opened his mouth obediently and gave over his loot, which he'd retrieved from a small trash can beside the dryer.

"Chance," the boys squealed again, as they realized he'd stepped into the kitchen behind her. In unison they exclaimed, "You came!" and launched themselves at him.

Laughing, he caught them and swept them up, one in each arm. "I told you I would, didn't I?" he asked, looking from one to the other.

Lynn had never seen a more beautiful sight than her boys gazing at him with looks so full of love and admiration that it made her heart sing. This was what it was all about. This was the desire of her heart.

"Don't cry, Momma," Jack said, reaching a hand out to her. "You can hug us, too."

Gavin reached out to her, too, and Chance crossed the gap between them and instantly she was engulfed into the center of the group hug. No. The family hug...

Chance kissed her gently and both boys squealed, nearly breaking her eardrums.

"Are you gonna be our daddy?" Gavin asked.

"Yeah," Jack said. "We didn't put you on our list for Santa Claus. We asked God fer you."

Chance gave her his slow, cocky grin. "That depends on your momma. What do you say, Lynn?"

"Say yes, Momma," Gavin whispered, his heart in his eyes.

Jack touched her cheek, his dark brows dipped over serious, imploring eyes. "Yes, Momma. Ain'tcha in love with 'im?"

Chance hiked a brow. "I like the way you boys think. But guys, your momma needs more time."

"No!" she exclaimed, and all three guys' expressions crashed. "I mean, no, I don't need more time. Yes, I love you and I'll marry you."

Both boys let out earsplitting yells of joy and Lynn knew, looking into Chance's beautiful, green eyes so full of love, that her life—and her hearing—would never be the same again.

"Now, can we go get a baby at the hospital?" Gavin asked, breaking the moment.

"Yeah," Jack agreed. "We asked Mr. Applegate why we couldn't have a baby like Tater and he said once y'all was married that the hospital would give us one."

Gavin grinned. "Tater's good. Miss Lacy said he don't cry none. So can we have one like him?"

Chance looked from one child to the next, then grinned, his eyes teasing. "Hey, I'm great with that. But let's get to the wedding first."

Lynn couldn't help it—she laughed. "I agree."

Chance set the boys down. "Guys, how about me and your momma talk dates for our wedding and then we'll meet y'all at the Christmas tree."

They nodded then raced toward the living room singing, "We're gettin' a tater tot, we're gettin' a tater tot!"

"I hope you know what you're doing!" Lynn said, as

he wrapped his arms around her waist and hauled her close, nuzzling her ear and sending her stomach into a spin and her nerves tingling.

"I know exactly what I'm doing. I'm planning on spending the rest of my life loving you."

"Good, I'm all in." She kissed him, slow and tenderly, and for the first time in a very long time she stepped out of the yaupon thicket and into clear pastures. It was a beautiful sight to behold.

Taking her hand, Chance led her toward the living room where their boys were waiting. "But just so you know," Lynn said, feeling lighthearted. "We are not naming our baby Tater Tot."

Chance winked at her. "That's okay, Lacy and Clint have dibs on that. Me personally, I like the ring of Spud Turner better.... Sounds like a rodeo champ to me."

Lynn laughed over the sound of her boy's happy chatter. "Oh, Chance," she said. "What a wonderful, wonderful life we are going to have—but if you think you are putting my boys on a bull you can forget about it."

"Darlin', we are in total agreement on all counts."

She laughed. "Not on all counts. Spud? Nope, we are not naming our child Spud."

"Then how about Idaho? That sounds good for the rodeo, too."

She laughed again. "Give it up, Chance."

At the word *rodeo* both boys stopped ogling their presents and spun. "We goin' to the rodeo?"

"Sure we are," Chance answered. "But not today. Right now we are going to sit down and I'm going to read to y'all about baby Jesus' birth like I promised."

"That sounds *good*," Jack cooed, and scrambled up

close to Chance as he sat down on Lynn's couch. Lynn smiled contently and thanked God once more for the blessings she'd been given. And she knew she was done holding on to her past.

Gavin grabbed his Bible storybook that he'd set on the coffee table in anticipation of Chance coming over, and then he crawled up to sit on Chance's other side. He handed over the book and then looked thoughtful.

"You think God thought about naming baby Jesus Tater?"

"I bet he did," Jack drawled. "It's a real good name. I like it!"

Lynn met Chance's dancing gaze over the top of Gavin's head and chuckled. "Are you sure you're ready for this? For us?"

Chance sobered. "Darlin', I've been ready my whole life for y'all."

* * * * *

Dear Reader,

Thank you for choosing to spend time with me and the Mule Hollow gang! I hope, as I always do, that you were able to put your feet up and relax while you visited my little town!

I loved writing the Men of Mule Hollow trilogy featuring the Turner men, and I couldn't wait all year long to get to Chance's book. Writing about a rodeo preacher appealed to me, and I could see Chance Turner was a cowboy preacher with a heart for God, winning souls of the rodeo cowboys to the Lord. But as always, I wondered what would shake him up…what would happen if circumstances changed and that way of life was taken from him. And also, what would happen when the right woman came along? Of course when questions like that hit my brain it means I have to write the story to get the answers. I hope you've enjoyed reading it as much as I did creating it.

People are always asking me how to get my earlier books, so I'm thrilled and excited that in March 2011 Love Inspired will be re-releasing my first two Mule Hollow books. They will be released together into a Love Inspired Classics two-in-one book. *The Trouble with Lacy Brown* and *And Baby Makes Five* are two of readers' all-time favorite Mule Hollow books. I hope if you haven't had the chance to visit Mule Hollow from its beginning that you'll pick one up. Or give it as a gift to a friend and introduce them to my stories.

Also, in May look for new Mule Hollow books as the fun continues!

And last but not least, as always, I love hearing from readers. You can reach me through my website, debraclopton.com, or my Facebook page or at P.O. Box 1125, Madisonville, Texas 77864.

Until next time, live, laugh and seek God with all your hearts.

Debra Clopton

QUESTIONS FOR DISCUSSION

1. I hope you enjoyed Chance and Lynn's story. If so, what about it did you enjoy the most? Why?

2. Lynn thought she was finally at peace with her life until Chance came crashing in. Why did his arrival open up all her old wounds and make her realize she was far from healed?

3. Chance had wounds of his own that he was trying to let heal. He thought coming to the solitude of the family ranch would be just what the doctor ordered...but God had different plans. Have you ever thought one thing was good for you and God showed you He had other plans for you? If so discuss this with the group.

4. Lynn couldn't trust men. And even though she knew Chance was an honorable, trustworthy man she still had a hard time. Even though she'd helped others move forward with their lives, she couldn't. Why?

5. Although Chance felt unworthy and deeply saddened, his life changed the moment he was run over by Lynn's twins, Gavin and Jack. There was no way he couldn't smile upon their first meeting. Do you ever feel sad and low and then God puts someone or something in your path that brightens

your day or changes your life for the better even though you didn't feel you deserved it?

6. Chance made his first big impression on Lynn when he promised her boys he'd watch them on the swing and then he actually did it. Why was this so important to her? As Christians, don't you believe the small things—or the seemingly small things—matter?

7. Why was it so important to Stacy to be married to Emmett by a preacher?

8. Why was it so important to Lynn for Chance to step up and be that preacher? I love seeing how God works in real life and in my books to bring people together in just the right moments—moments I call "God moments." Have you experienced "God moments?" Discuss these and their effects on you with the group.

9. Applegate and Stanley are pretty frank about the first preacher who came to preach at the church. What would you have done in their situation?

10. Chance was angry at God because he believed God should have given him one more chance to win Randy's soul. Then he remembered that God did give him that chance. When was it and what happened?

11. How did this help Chance?

12. What kind of life change do you think Chance will make in the lives of Lynn's twins?

13. The matchmakers saw the signs and pushed Lynn to bid on Chance in the auction. They wanted to make a difference in Lynn's and Chance's lives. Is there something you can do to help make a difference in someone's life?

TITLES AVAILABLE NEXT MONTH

Available December 28, 2010

HIS COUNTRY GIRL
The Granger Family Ranch
Jillian Hart

THE BABY PROMISE
Carolyne Aarsen

THE COWBOY'S FAMILY
Brenda Minton

SECOND CHANCE RANCH
Leann Harris

THE RANCHER'S REUNION
Tina Radcliffe

ROCKY MOUNTAIN HERO
Audra Harders

LICNM1210

REQUEST YOUR FREE BOOKS!

2 FREE INSPIRATIONAL NOVELS
PLUS 2
FREE
MYSTERY GIFTS

YES! Please send me 2 FREE Love Inspired® novels and my 2 FREE mystery gifts (gifts are worth about $10). After receiving them, if I don't wish to receive any more books, I can return the shipping statement marked "cancel." If I don't cancel, I will receive 6 brand-new novels every month and be billed just $4.24 per book in the U.S. or $4.74 per book in Canada. That's a saving of over 20% off the cover price. It's quite a bargain! Shipping and handling is just 50¢ per book.* I understand that accepting the 2 free books and gifts places me under no obligation to buy anything. I can always return a shipment and cancel at any time. Even if I never buy another book, the two free books and gifts are mine to keep forever.

105/305 IDN E7PP

Name   (PLEASE PRINT)

Address   Apt. #

City   State/Prov.   Zip/Postal Code

Signature (if under 18, a parent or guardian must sign)

Mail to Steeple Hill Reader Service:

IN U.S.A.: P.O. Box 1867, Buffalo, NY 14240-1867
IN CANADA: P.O. Box 609, Fort Erie, Ontario L2A 5X3

Not valid for current subscribers to Love Inspired books.

Want to try two free books from another series?
Call 1-800-873-8635 or visit www.morefreebooks.com.

* Terms and prices subject to change without notice. Prices do not include applicable taxes. N.Y. residents add applicable sales tax. Canadian residents will be charged applicable provincial taxes and GST. Offer not valid in Quebec. This offer is limited to one order per household. All orders subject to approval. Credit or debit balances in a customer's account(s) may be offset by any other outstanding balance owed by or to the customer. Please allow 4 to 6 weeks for delivery. Offer available while quantities last.

Your Privacy: Steeple Hill Books is committed to protecting your privacy. Our Privacy Policy is available online at www.SteepleHill.com or upon request from the Reader Service. From time to time we make our lists of customers available to reputable third parties who may have a product or service of interest to you. If you would prefer we not share your name and address, please check here. ☐

Help us get it right—We strive for accurate, respectful and relevant communications. To clarify or modify your communication preferences, visit us at www.ReaderService.com/consumerchoice.

LIREG10R

When Texas Ranger Benjamin Fritz arrives at his captain's house after receiving an urgent message, he finds him murdered and the man's daughter in shock.

Read on for a sneak peek at DAUGHTER OF TEXAS by Terri Reed, the first book in the exciting new TEXAS RANGER JUSTICE *series, available January 2011 from Love Inspired Suspense.*

Corinna's dark hair had loosened from her normally severe bun. And her dark eyes were glassy as she stared off into space. Taking her shoulders in his hands, Ben pulled her to her feet. She didn't resist. He figured shock was setting in.

When she turned to face him, his heart contracted painfully in his chest. "You're hurt!"

She didn't seem to hear him.

Blood seeped from a scrape on her right upper biceps. He inspected the wound. Looked as if a bullet had grazed her. Whoever had killed her father had tried to kill her. With aching ferocity, rage roared through Ben. The heat of the bullet cauterized the flesh. It would probably heal quickly enough.

But Ben had a feeling that her heart wouldn't heal any time soon. She'd adored her father. That had been apparent from the moment Ben set foot in the Pike world. She'd barely tolerated Ben from the get-go, with her icy stare and brusque manner, making it clear she thought him not good enough to be in her world. But when it came to her father...

Greg had known that if anything happened to him, she'd need help coping with the loss.

Ben, I need you to promise me if anything ever happens to me, you'll watch out for Corinna. She'll need an anchor fear she's too fragile to suffer another death.

Of course Ben had promised. Though he'd refused to even allow the thought to form that any harm would befall his mentor and friend. He'd wanted to believe Greg was indestructible. But he wasn't. None of them were.

The Rangers were human and very mortal, performing a risky job that put their lives on the line every day.

Never before had Ben been so acutely aware of that fact.

Now his captain was gone. It was up to him not only to bring Greg's murderer to justice, but to protect and help Corinna Pike.

*For more of this story, look for DAUGHTER OF TEXAS
by Terri Reed, available in January 2011
from Love Inspired Suspense.*